The author welcomes comments and questions. Please visit www. LarryJacobson.com

Published by:

BUOY
—PRESS—

Emeryville, California
Www.BuoyPress.com
Info@BuoyPress.com

ISBN: 978-0-9828787-0-5

"LET'S GO!"

Written by: Larry Jacobson

Edited by: Cate Hogan

Cover and illustrations by:
Vladimir Cebu

Let's Go! Is based on the true story of two young men who circumnavigated in a sailboat.

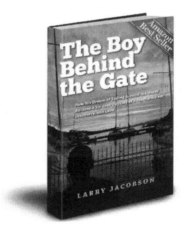

DEDICATION

Dedicated to John van Duyl. You brought my writing from dark to light and your encouragement made this book become a reality. Your friendship will be remembered forever. Rest in peace.

1951-2019

Table of Contents

CHAPTER 0—THE ENVELOPE...1

CHAPTER 1—THE ODD BOY OUT 5

CHAPTER 2—SKIP GETS HIS FEET WET...................................11

CHAPTER 3—SKIP LEARNS ABOUT HARD WORK................. 17

CHAPTER 4—SKIP'S BROKEN HEART.......................................23

CHAPTER 5—AUNT BEATRICE? NO WAY!.............................27

CHAPTER 6—YOU CAN'T GO YET..31

CHAPTER 7—DOES THIS OCEAN EVER END?.........................39

CHAPTER 8—SKIP MEETS KANEK..47

CHAPTER 9—THE SEARCH BEGINS..55

CHAPTER 10—THE WORST PASSAGE EVER—AND THE
BEST...71

CHAPTER 11—CROCODILES, SNAKES, AND JELLYFISH
EWW!... 81

CHAPTER 12—ISLAND OF THE DRAGONS.............................87

CHAPTER 13—THE CLOSEST CALL OF ALL......................... 101

CHAPTER 14—CAMELS AND OIL.. 113

CHAPTER 15 —PIRATES!... 123

CHAPTER 16—WHY THE RED SEA IS BLUE...........................129

CHAPTER 17—CREEPY PLACES 137

CHAPTER 18 — THE UNDERWATER CITY...............................145

CHAPTER 19—THE BIG DECISION..157

CHAPTER 20—A NEW CLUE.. 163

CHAPTER 21—OPEN THE GATES!.. 169

CHAPTER 22—WHICH WAY? 175

GLOSSARY... 181

CHAPTER 0—THE ENVELOPE

"And to my beloved Skip," the lawyer read aloud. Skip sat staring into space, his eyes moist and sad. He was lost in a distant past world—the only world he had ever been happy in—a world where his only true friend, his mother was alive. She was everything to him and now he felt empty, without hope or joy, and without purpose.

The attorney continued reading Julia's last will and testament. "Skip, you have always had big dreams and have worked hard toward those dreams. Never give up on those dreams Skip. Now that I'm gone, they're even more important to your life. You've taken your little old mother out on plenty of sailing trips. But I know you, and you're surely looking for a bigger boat. You didn't know your father very well, but he sure loved you and worked hard to provide for us. There was no need for you to know before this, but your father's investments have done very well and he's left us enough to be comfortable for quite a while. And if you're reading this and I'm gone, then it all goes to you Skip. There's enough money here for you to make your dreams come true. Dreaming is only the first step though Skip. You must take action because dreams require work to make them reality. Whatever you do, know I shall be with you forever and will be there when you need strength and encouragement. Go Skip, Go!

P.S. Now you may read the envelope the attorney is handing you."

"There's an envelope here for you," said the attorney. "It's marked private," he said as he handed Skip the sealed envelope. Skip hesitated, then slowly peeled the envelope open. He read the same one page letter over and over again, trying to comprehend what it all meant.

At the lawyer's office

"Dear Skip,

I haven't told you this story before because I didn't want to add more stress to your life. But now that I'm gone, you should know, you have a brother. He's almost twice your age and he has had his share of troubles. We adopted him as an infant refugee and all we knew about him was that he comes from somewhere on a remote Pacific Island. They told us his name was Boy of the Moon but we thought he would want something shorter, so for no real reason, we called him Brian. He was born with a crescent moon shaped birthmark on his lower right leg.

Brian and your father were very close. When your father died, Brian was devastated. He got in with the wrong crowd and then got into some trouble with the law. While he was out on bail, Brian ran away and has been gone ever since. The last time we heard from him was on these two postcards from Tahiti. The first one says he's okay, and that he's looking for his birthplace. The second one is a couple of months later and just says, "THE LEGEND LIVES. MoonBoy rises." I don't know what he meant by this, and hope he's safe.

Find your brother Skip.

Love,

Mom"

Skip was in a daze. He stood up, walked out of the lawyer's office and kept walking. He walked until he could walk no more, then flopped face down on the grass in the park trying to make sense of it all. *With Mom gone, what's left for me here? All the kids at school hate me. Maybe I should leave....* Thoughts began swirling around in Skip's head and suddenly he sat upright. *Maybe I should sail to Tahiti to find my brother Brian, and then he and I could sail around the world! Or we could come home and Brian could beat up the bullies. A big brother? That would be so cool. I bet he'd never make fun of me. But how? I don't know where to begin, what to do, Mom, I'm so confused!* Skip's whole world seemed to collapse and explode at the same time as he fell fast asleep on the grass.

CHAPTER 1—THE ODD BOY OUT

Maybe today would be a little different. Maybe the bullies wouldn't pick on Skip. Maybe they wouldn't give him boogies, noogies, or a wedgie, steal his lunch, or poke him in his stomach. He hoped the bus would arrive before the bullies did so he'd at least be in a safe zone for the ride to school. Skip dreaded going to school with his so-called friends. Why did they have to be so mean? Why couldn't they just leave him alone? Skip knew he was in for another day of it as Bruce and Mike shouted from a distance, "Hey, why don't you throw yourself in front of the bus so the driver doesn't have to use the brakes! Skip just did what he did every day, he ignored the other kids. He couldn't wait to get out of this grade and meet new friends—maybe ones he actually liked.

Skip's short hair was always in a crew cut and this made his slightly round face look plump as if he always had his cheeks full of food like a squirrel. This was often true as he couldn't seem to stop snacking on anything, from chips to nuts. At 12 years old, he stood average height but more than average width. He was about 30 pounds too heavy, which made him a terrible runner. Not only did his fat jiggle as he ran, but even when he walked, which was more like a waddle. Because of this, he never ran anywhere and he was always teased at school when he played sports because he was so slow. Some of the other kids had nicknamed him "Jello" which made him hate running even more. Even his gym teacher at school yelled, "C'mon Jello, see if you can make it to first

5

base!" Of course that was only if he got a hit in baseball, which was rare. Usually he just sat on the bench staring out into space dreaming. He did this in class too. His teacher often caught him staring out the window and nicknamed him "Dreamer."

"What are you staring at Skip?" Mrs. Rockland had queried one day.

"Oh, nothing really, it's just peaceful and quiet out there is all," answered Skip. His habit of staring with a blank look out the window, otherwise known as daydreaming, had started four years ago after his father had died of cancer. Skip had been close with his dad and they used to practice baseball almost every day after his dad came home from work. Skip would be waiting on the porch with his baseball mitt and ball ready to go as soon as his dad walked up the driveway. Skip wasn't actually all that bad at throwing and catching, but it didn't come natural to him like it did to his dad. He stopped practicing when his father was no longer around to play with him. He missed his dad, and couldn't seem to find a friend at school he could trust or who cared about him like his dad did. As time went by, Skip became closer with his Mom as he saw what a good friend she was as well as a loving mother. Being an only child was hard enough, and he felt like an outcast because he was chubby and wasn't interested in the same things as the other kids. He always felt like the odd boy out but didn't really understand why. He did know that someday he would show them all what he could do...after he figured out just what that was. In the meantime, he often came home from school depressed and would run up to his room and stay there until dinner. He never cried actual tears, but instead got angry and he let his anger grow inside like a volcano building up pressure. He wasn't sure who he was angry at, but he knew why. He was angry for his messed up childhood without a dad, his fat stomach, and his flat feet that made that horrible "flop-flop" sound that someone always noticed when he ran. Skip hated being bullied. One day on his walk home, he couldn't take it anymore and started shouting back at Bruce and Mike, the two boys who were constantly teasing him. The boys were just about to pounce on him when suddenly, Skip shouted at the top of his lungs, "No more bullies!" and charged straight at the boys like a mad bull. It seemed that all of Skip's anger was released in his first punch as he pounded Bruce into the sidewalk. But Mike grabbed Skip from behind and wrestled him to the ground where both he and Bruce had the advantage. After a couple of minutes of beating up on Skip, the two bullies turned and ran away. As they ran, Skip sat up, wiped his bloody nose, and shouted back at them, "No more bullies!" *"Someday, Skip thought...someday I'll show them what I can do. No more bullies."*

While Skip didn't like the nicknames given by the teasing kids, he did like his name, "Skip." His mom Julia said she had named him Skip because he made her so happy, she wanted to skip down the sidewalk. It was only a few years ago he learned to skip rocks on the water and felt he was living up to his namesake. He was pretty good at it too, and had skipped some flat rocks as many as 12 times along the surface of the water.

Skip lived up to his name

CHAPTER 1 – THE ODD BOY OUT

Skip lived a few miles from the beach in sunny southern California. His skin turned light brown from the sun, and he often smelled like coconut because of the suntan lotion he used. He went to the beach every weekend during the summer. The ocean was Skip's saving grace and he spent so much time in the water he became a good swimmer and since fat floats more than muscle, he had no worries about sinking. He was comfortable around the water and felt like the other kids couldn't touch him while he was swimming or floating in the ocean. His mom loved to swim in the ocean too, and every Saturday morning during the summer, she and Skip would clamber into the car along with picnic baskets, beach towels, and a watermelon—always a watermelon. Once they were ready, the two beach-goers turned to each other and shouted in unison, "Let's go!" and off they'd go, giggling all the way to the shore.

Julia and Skip would sit at the water's edge and laugh and giggle while spitting watermelon seeds as the waves splashed over them. Sometimes they built sand castles together and other times they just talked. Skip always had questions for his mom and she patiently answered his eager questions about the world. His curious mind never seemed to take a rest—all of that daydreaming was really the sign of a very quick mind that was never satisfied. Skip always seemed to be searching for "the answer" but still wasn't even sure what the question was.

Most of the other 12-year old's at the beach thought Skip was weird because he was so quiet and to make matters worse, he dressed in what he thought were cool clothes, but were really a fashion accident. He wore checkered surf trunks, a red and white striped t-shirt which showed off his chubby belly, and red tennis shoes. It never really occurred to him what he was wearing though, and he didn't spend much time worrying about it.

One day at the beach, while Skip was staring out at the ocean, he saw a boat gliding along ever so smoothly as it made its way through the blue water that sparkled with golden rays from the sun. Skip stared at the boat, then turned to his mom and asked, "Why don't I hear the motor noise? How does that boat move without a motor?" Julia patiently explained, "The wind is pushing on the boat's sails and it needs no other power." Skip couldn't believe his eyes as he silently watched the boat sail away over the horizon until he couldn't see it anymore. "Mom! Where did it go? Why can't I see the boat anymore?"

Julia answered patiently again, "Perhaps it's sailing across the ocean to distant lands. Maybe it's going to sail all the way around the world."

"Can you do that? Can you sail around the world?" asked the now very curious Skip.

"Sure you can Skip, you can do anything you set your mind to," Julia said. This private time with his mom at the beach was his favorite time of all. She patiently explained that the earth was round so if you set sail east or west, and you sail long enough, you'll end up back where you started. Skip's mind raced, and then in one of those "a-ha" moments of discovery, he had the answer to what he was gazing at all of the time. He wasn't looking blankly into space, he was staring adventure in the face.

He stood at the water's edge for a long time, looking fixedly at the boat as it disappeared into the setting western sun. Skip didn't talk much on the ride home that day, which was unusual for him, as he was now deep in thought with ideas of what it would be like to cross the oceans. Was it like the movies he had seen on TV? Were there beautiful white sand beaches? Treacherous pirates? Giant monsters? Big storms? Whirlpools that swallowed up big ships? *"I bet no one would tease me out there,"* Skip thought to himself.

For the first time in as long as he could remember, Skip had a glimmer of hope. Until now his unhappy life seemed destined to continue the way it was with every day more miserable than the next. While he didn't have much hope in his current life, maybe he could find it "out there." From that hot summer day on, all Skip could talk about was sailboats and how he was going to get his own boat. And he paid the price for that with his friends. Now they called him "Popeye the Jello-sailor man."

CHAPTER 2—SKIP GETS HIS FEET WET

Even though Skip had never been in a sailboat, he was now fascinated by them. Skip spent a lot of time alone, and he read magazines and books he checked out of the school library— all about explorers, voyagers, and boating. His iPad was nearly filled with pictures of boats sailing on turquoise blue waters and while he didn't study much for his school classes, he was picking up a pretty good knowledge of sailing vocabulary. It was like learning a whole new language and it thrilled him because it was a language nobody else at school understood. From all of his reading, even though he still hadn't sailed, Skip felt he knew the workings of a boat and even the basics of adjusting the sails. It was one more element of his life that separated him from the rest of the kids, and he liked that none of them had a clue what he was talking about when he spoke about boats.

He read about the fearless explorers who, against all odds, set sail on their voyages of discovery. He got to know Christopher Columbus, one of the first Europeans to discover America by accident because he thought he had reached the shores of the East Indies. Then he read about Magellan and Drake, both who led expeditions that made it all the way around the world by sailboat. And of course there was his favorite, Captain James Cook, the great sailor, navigator, and explorer of the vast Pacific Ocean.

One day Skip came zooming up to his house on his bicycle shouting, "Mom! Mom! Hurry! I found it! I found it!" Julia, who was almost always in the kitchen, had been baking chocolate chip cookies. She came running out of the kitchen wiping her hands on her apron.

"What on earth are you talking about," asked Julia. "Calm down, calm down, now tell me." Skip had found the **hull** of a little sailboat hull in a garbage dumpster and wanted Julia to drive him over to pick it up with their big Chevy station wagon. "Please mom, please," Skip pleaded. I'll paint it and fix it up and I'll do more chores to pay for a sail and then I can sail everywhere! Pleeeeese Mom?" Julia gave in easily and soon they were unloading the old 8-foot hull of the most basic of beginner boats. It may have been junked by the previous owner, but to Skip it looked like a super yacht.

Julia had never seen Skip so passionate about anything as much as his boat. He sanded and varnished and painted, then sanded and painted some more until finally he announced the hull was ready. To pay for the materials, he did extra chores around the house and then got a job mowing neighbors' lawns. He saved enough money to buy a sail and the rigging to go with it. Skip had himself a boat. When he showed his mother, he beamed with pride and she gave him the biggest hug any mom ever gave to their son.

He taught himself how to sail, and sailed that little boat every day he could. One day, he even sailed the two miles across the bay to the island of Avalonia. He was so proud when he landed his boat on the island! He walked along the beach looking at seashells and skipping rocks, and then he plopped down on the beach and fell asleep feeling ever so good about his accomplishment.

Skip awoke with a start as the sound of strong wind whipped the sail loudly and rocked his boat back and forth on the beach. He stared out at the water in fear—was this the same water he had just crossed? Instead of calm seas and gentle breezes, the wind had built and was kicking up **whitecaps** on the bay and the waves were too big to see over the tops. He couldn't even make out the mainland because the wind was blowing such heavy mist through the air. His only choices were to stay on the little island or hurry up and launch his boat back on the water and point toward home before the wind got even stronger. Suddenly, he felt a chill race all through his body—Skip he was afraid. Nobody knew he had sailed to Avalonia and he just had to get back before his mom got worried. Skip didn't have enough experience yet to know that where he lived on the coast, the wind came up stronger every day in the afternoon. Then in the evening, the winds would die down and it would become calm again. He could have simply waited until the winds calmed down and had a nice sail home. But he was scared, and without experience how was he to know?

The little boat with its red and white sail **bucked and bobbed, listed, and lurched, broached and yawed,** and Skip thought he nearly capsized in the big waves. He hadn't realized how powerful the water could be. Skip started to shake uncontrollably. "Oh, what am I doing?! Why am I doing this? Now I'm probably going to die!" The wind blew the water over the **bow**, sending the salt stinging into his face. His hands hurt from holding tight to the **sheets** that controlled the sail. He thought, "This is it, I'm never going to make it!" He pictured his mother at home in the kitchen cooking a delicious hot supper with plenty of broccoli. He wondered how long it would be before anybody realized he was gone forever. Oh, why did I do this? I can't sail! I'm a fat lump of Jello.

Skip gets his feet wet and has a close call

Slowly, an image appeared out of the mist. It was as tall as the clouds and loomed with great power in front of the boat. It was a tall man with curly white hair wearing a blue naval jacket with gold buttons and embroidery over a white shirt with ruffles. Skip blinked and shook his head at what he was seeing and now hearing from this image. "Skip, it's Captain James Cook. Hang on Skip! There's always an end to every passage, ease the sheets, concentrate on keeping the boat afloat and you'll be fine," and then the image faded away. Captain James Cook! Skip's idol! *Well, do what he says, Skip said out loud to himself.* Skip eased the sheets, turned off the wind a little, and leveled the boat off. *Cook made it through storms bigger than this and kept going, why can't I? I can. I'm not washing up on that sand like a beached whale! I can do this!*

Skip forced himself onward. His arms ached from holding the main sheet and rudder, but he didn't let go. His fingers were turning blue, but he didn't' care. He held on. The salt stung his eyes, but he kept them open and glued to the coastline as it appeared out of the mist. 'C'mon, not much farther now,' he kept telling himself as he willed himself to concentrate on the boat. After what seemed like forever, he arrived back at the shore where he had started this epic day of adventure. He flopped out of the boat onto the sand exhausted, his arms sore, his blue fingers slowly coming back to life, his body soaking wet, and his face covered in salt. And his smile stretched from ear to ear. He had made it. Skip had completed his very first voyage and had become a sailor. Or so he thought.

When he came home very, very late, he nearly shouted, "Mom, Mom! I did it! I sailed to Avalonia and back!" He told her about Captain Cook talking to him and Julia nodded in understanding. "Well, now you have a new friend, that's good," she said calmly. Instead of scolding him, she waited for the right moment so she wouldn't spoil his excitement, and said, "Next time, if you tell me where you're going, then I won't worry." She knew there would always be a next time.

"Mom, I should just tell you now." Skip stood up, squared his shoulders back and boldly announced, "Mom, I, Captain Skip am going to sail around the world." She could see it in his eyes. She could see the passion and determination, and she knew he would overcome any obstacle put in his way until he had achieved his dream. "I believe you will, Captain Skip," said Julia. Skip was beaming with pride and marched around the kitchen with his head held high like Captain Cook.

Things are looking up, Skip thought as he fantasized about an exotic life in distant lands. Little did he know his dreams were about to shatter.

CHAPTER 3—SKIP LEARNS ABOUT HARD WORK

"**M**om, I need a bigger boat. How am I going to sail all the way around the world without a bigger boat?"

"Big boats are expensive dear," his mother replied. "You might have to save for a long time before you can buy one. But look how your first boat arrived. You had your eyes and ears open and were thinking about boats. That tells the world what you're thinking and what you want. I don't know how it works, but it does. You know there's a famous writer and poet, Ralph Waldo Emerson. He was also a modern day philosopher and said, 'Once you make a decision, the universe conspires to make it happen.' I think maybe he was right, don't you?"

"And then think of how hard you work, and all the good things you do for other people. I'm convinced the more good you do, the more good things come back to you. The world has a tendency to want to remain in balance. I think if you do enough good things for others, treat people kindly, and be a contributor for good in the world, then maybe, just maybe, your big boat will come to you."

Skip decided he would do everything he could to help others so his big boat would show up someday. He worked hard pulling weeds and mowing lawns in his neighborhood, he also took another job on weekends cleaning boats in the boat yard. One day he shuffled into the kitchen covered in dirt with a frown on his face, looked up into Julia's wise eyes and asked, "Mom, I've been working hard and helping others and still my boat hasn't shown up. I just spent all day working in Mrs. Gerstein's garden and have been running so many errands for people that I'm starting to be called 'errand boy.' And still, my big boat is nowhere to be seen. Are you sure it will happen?" Julia was standing at the stove, stirring her big pot of bubbling chicken soup as it wafted homey smells of potato, chicken, and fresh chopped onion and garlic through the house. A second steaming pot was piled high with what looked like enough broccoli to feed the whole block. She stopped, wiped her hands on her apron, put her arm around Skip and sat with him at the kitchen table. Her wise eyes were penetrating and warm, and always made Skip feel so loved. Skip noticed the cat scratch scar on her left cheek had turned into three little white stripes with her summer suntan. The scar from Aunt Beatrice's cat looked permanent.

"I know you've been working hard Skip. And I know you've been helping others. Even Mrs. Gerstein down the street called and told me what a good boy you've been working in her garden and picking up her groceries for her. And I know you've been expecting your boat to show up. But it doesn't work like that. You're working and helping others so you can get your boat. You're doing that for you. But remember when you're doing things for others and expecting something in return, you're not really giving, you're working for payment. To truly give generously means to give with no expectations. Just do it out of the goodness of your heart, and because you want to help them. Do you see the difference?"

"I don't get it." said Skip with puzzled eyes.

Julia replied with her warm soft voice, "Because my dear, when you give to others, you should be giving to help them, not you." Then she leaped up out of her chair shouting, "The broccoli!" and ran to the stove to turn the flame down to simmer.

Skip's mom Julia in the kitchen. "The broccoli!"

Skip sat for a while pondering what his mother had told him, and he began connecting the dots. The other day Mrs. Gerstein was admiring her rose garden and told Skip that thanks to him, her roses had never looked so beautiful. He had felt a warm fuzzy feeling, and it made him stand up a little taller. It was the same feeling he got when helping his mom. He knew that with his new understanding of helping others, his big boat would be arriving soon and he had better be ready. He jumped up from the kitchen table and went to his room where he began to pack for his sailing trip around the world. Later that night, as Skip was closing his eyes to sleep, he saw a small bright light on the ceiling. He gaped in awe as he watched the light grow larger and brighter. It grew into a head of white curly hair while the rest of Captain James Cook slowly took shape. He hovered on the ceiling looking down at Skip without saying anything for what seemed like a long time, but was only a few seconds. Finally, he nodded his head at Skip and said, "Good night, Captain," and was gone in a flash. Skip didn't sleep much that night.

In the late summer afternoons, Skip would ride his bike down to the bay to go for a sail in his little boat. When he was through sailing for the day he would hop on his bike and ride over to the marina where the big boats were docked. The gangways were always locked so he stood behind the gate staring at the yachts. After a few minutes, he closed his eyes and could see himself at the wheel, backing out of the slip, heading out the channel, turning south, and sailing away. Skip didn't want to be the boy behind the gate. He wanted to be at the helm calling, "Cast off the dock lines, I'm headed to sea."

Skip's bag remained packed and it sat right where he left it for what seemed to him like an eternity. In reality it was only a few months later when again he had questions for his mother while she was in the kitchen. This time she was busy setting the dinner table for the relatives who were arriving shortly, including Skip's least favorite, Aunt Beatrice. But no matter how Julia was, she always made time to answer Skip's questions. "Yes, Skip, what is it?"

"Mom, I've been working so hard and saving for my boat. And I've been working so hard to help others, and like you said, I've been doing it for them, not me. When's my boat gonna arrive?"

20

"Help me with the silverware dear," Julia said as she scurried about. "I know you think you've worked hard enough, and given enough of your heart, your soul, and your time. But dear, do you remember when you sailed to Avalonia?"

"Yeah"…said Skip, "What's that have to do with it?"

"Well, did you stop half way and say, "That's far enough, I don't want to sail any longer? No, you kept going all the way to Avalonia and then you sailed all the way back. You completed your voyage, didn't you?"

"Yes Mom."

"Then keep at it Skip. Be patient. Your turn will come and so will your boat. You can hang onto a dream for a long time. Never let go of your dreams." She reached over and gave Skip a big hug and said, "I love you, my dear Skip."

"I love you too mom." Julia was more than his mom—Julia was Skip's best friend.

All of a sudden Julia threw her hands in the air and shouted, "The broccoli!" while laughing at the water boiling over onto the stove.

CHAPTER 4— SKIP'S BROKEN HEART

He swung open the screen door and shouted, "Mom, I'm home! Mom! Mom?" Skip heard voices—lots of voices—coming from the living room. Peeking around the corner, he saw dozens of people—some familiar faces—and some not. What was going on? Were they having a party he had forgotten about? He walked in and said, "Hey everybody, what's going on? Where's Mom?"

"Come here Skip, said Aunt Beatrice. Tears were streaming down her cheeks, and as Skip surveyed the room, he realized everybody had tears on their face. The whole room was crying!

"What's going on?" Skip said, then he shouted, "What's going on?! Where's Mom!? The room fell silent. Where is she?! Somebody tell me what's going on!"

Beatrice held onto Skip's shoulders, looked him square in the eyes and said, "There's been an accident. Your mother was in a car accident."

"Is she okay? Where is she? In the hospital? I want to go see her!" Skip shouted. Beatrice held Skip firmly and quietly whispered, "Skip, your mother didn't survive the accident."

"No. No! No!!! Noooooooooooooooooooo!" Skip screamed. "I don't believe you!" He broke loose from his aunt's grip and looked around the room. Skip felt cold. He turned and walked silently out the front door and kept walking, stopping only when his short legs couldn't go on anymore and he collapsed onto the grass in the park. Face down, he pounded the ground with his fists and cried. He cried for his mom, he cried for himself, and he cried for all of the days he had wanted to cry in the past. He cried until he ran out of tears and could cry no more, and then passed out from exhaustion.

Skip cried until he ran out of tears

It was long past dark when Skip walked home shivering in the cold night air. Everything looked cold and black to him. The sky was black, the houses were dark and ominous, and even the once-green trees had turned to silhouettes. Skip's whole world had faded to darkness.

CHAPTER 5—AUNT BEATRICE? NO WAY!

S kip was in a daze. He stood up, walked out of the lawyer's office and kept walking. He walked until he could walk no more, then flopped face down on the grass in the park trying to make sense of it all. *With Mom gone, what's left for me here? All the kids at school hate me. Maybe I should leave....* Thoughts began swirling around in Skip's head and suddenly he sat upright. *maybe I should sail to Tahiti to find my brother Brian, and then he and I could sail around the world! Now? At my age? I don't know where to begin, what to do, Mom, I'm so confused! Skip's whole world seemed to collapse and explode at the same time as he fell fast asleep on the grass.*

Skip didn't know how much longer he could take living with Aunt Beatrice. She wasn't mean but she was WEIRD. Everybody knew Beatrice was a little cuckoo. She lived in Encino with her 11 cats, four dogs, a turtle, two hamsters, a guinea pig, and four ducks. She collected picnic baskets and they were everywhere in the house and came in all sizes and shapes; big ones, little ones, round ones, square ones, tall ones, and short mini ones. Every time she would go somewhere, along came a picnic basket and in it would be her awful home baked fruitcake. She smelled of cheap perfume, wore clothes from the 1970's and played nonstop disco music on her record player with scratched vinyl records.

And on top of that, from noon on every day, she flitted around the house with a drink in her hand singing, "At the discotheque, at the discotheque, crying at the discotheque…" while she danced with some imaginary dance partner. She never cooked and Skip became the house chef, maid, errand boy, and was loaded down with a heavy load of chores. He hardly had time for school, let alone homework. Skip began asking himself what he was still doing at Aunt Beatrice's house.

Skip figured if he wasn't going to school anyway, he may as well do what he wanted, and that was to set out on his quest to find his brother Brian. It was all he thought about and he often stared at a map of the pacific ocean pinned up on his wall. The island of Tahiti was marked "Brian." He turned the two post cards over and over again in his hands, studying Brian's face intently and scrutinizing every so closely the crescent moon birthmark on his leg. He had to go find his brother, and surely Brian would want to be with him too…right? He would under-stand Skip, and Skip would understand him. Slowly but surely, Skip worked to put his plan into place. He wouldn't run away. No, he would *sail* away!

Slowly, the plan to sail away was hatched. Over the next few months, Skip tolerated being at Aunt Beatrice's but he remembered what his mom had told him over and over again. "Accept or reject, don't tolerate." Skip knew that meant if he wasn't happy with his situation, he had to be the one to change things or they would stay the same. Skip stopped talking about his plan with anybody else and Aunt Beatrice had just waved off his sailing adventure as a kid's daydream.

But in the meantime, Skip had arranged with the attorney to get enough money out of his inheritance to look for a boat to buy. He finally found a good used boat that was somewhat seaworthy. The boat (she) needed a lot of work and Skip decided he could do most of it, and at least help the experts when they came to fix the electronics, some plumbing, rigging, and mechanical issues. Skip watched and learned and asked lots of questions. He sanded and painted, and cleaned and polished until his hands were too sore to go on. Skip spent less time daydreaming and instead studied how all of the systems on the boat worked. He took her out sailing on weekends and learned to sail her with pretty good confi-dence. And late into every night he studied books about cruising routes so he knew when the right time was to cross the Pacific ocean to Tahiti, and beyond. Half a year later, Skip felt ready.

CHAPTER 6—YOU CAN'T GO YET

S kip was sweating, his arms ached, and his legs could barely take another step. He had been counting and this was his 14th trip carrying groceries and supplies to the boat. He had been busy working to get ready for months and now he was finally putting fresh food aboard for his departure the next day.

"Hey, where you headed to young man?" asked the grey-haired gentleman on the dock, known only as Mr. Grey. "That's a lot of food and supplies for a weekend getaway!"

"I'm not going for just the weekend Mr. Grey, I'm going to Tahiti to find my lost brother."

"You have a lost brother? If he's lost, how are you going to find him?" Skip told him the story of Moon Boy and how he ran away to find his birthplace on an island in the South Pacific, and that's why he was headed to Tahiti.

"Well, that's quite a story young man. But are you ready to cross the Pacific ocean? Do you have enough experience and do you have the knowledge?" asked the old man.

Skip stood as tall as he could, squared his shoulders, and stepped toward the man. "Mr. Grey, do you ever go sailing? I know you have a boat here, but I've never ever seen you take it out of the slip. I'm not going to take sailing advice from someone who doesn't sail." Skip turned to walk away, but then stopped, swung around and added in too harsh a tone, "And I don't need to know everything to go sailing. I'll learn as I go!" Clearly, Skip was tired of hearing people tell him all the reasons he wouldn't succeed at sailing to Tahiti. After all, he was now almost 13 years old and felt that was old enough. However, he seemed to be the only one with that opinion as everybody he told at school laughed at him, thought he was nuts, and told him he would surely end up disappearing to the bottom of the deep blue sea.

The next morning, Skip left the dock and headed out to sea. It was hard to pinpoint just what he felt that morning but his mind was all over the place. Was he afraid? Oh yes, very afraid of what he would encounter on his trip. And he was nervous about how he would handle it too. He thought of Captain Cook and wondered if he too had been afraid…of course he had. It was natural to be afraid. Skip didn't feel sad to be leaving Aunt Beatrice and hoped she would understand when she read his note explaining how he had to go find his brother. More than anything, he was looking forward to a life without being teased and without people pre-judging him based only on his chubby belly. Even though every person he knew told him not to go, he could still hear his mom's words of encouragement and that gave him strength. She would have been the one person to say, "Go."

Because it was so early in the morning, the wind hadn't come up yet and Skip was motoring his boat out to sea. After he had gone no more than about four miles, he felt a slight breeze on his cheek. It was time to put up the sails. But just as he reached down to turn off the engine, he heard a noise that didn't sound right. The diesel engine, which was cooled by water, normally made a "whoosh" sound as the water was blown out the exhaust. But instead of whooshing, it sounded like it was coughing…more like a dry throat than the smooth liquid sound. When he looked over the stern, he waited to see the usual water shooting out of the exhaust. But the coughing only got louder and suddenly Skip realized there was no longer any water cooling the engine! Without knowing much about motors, he had no idea why this was happening, but he knew enough to recognize a problem when he saw one—water had to come in, circulate through the engine, and then exit—that's what kept the engine cool. Otherwise it would overheat and blow up! Skip shut the engine down and the boat came to a stop in the calm morning water. *"Now what?"* he thought. Skip needed his engine. Without it, how would he charge his batteries, operate electronics, GPS, and motor into anchorages? Without mechanical knowledge, Skip didn't know where, or what to look for in order to repair the engine.

Reluctantly, Skip continued the process of raising his sails, then turned the boat around 180 degrees, and headed back to port under sail. A couple of hours later, Skip sailed up to the same dock he had left that morning, tied the boat up, and sat slumped in the cockpit. A few minutes later, Mr. Grey walked by. He wasn't mean like Skip expected, but instead said, "Skip, I know you want to sail to Tahiti, but we all suffer setbacks. It's part of life you know, you'll just have to start again. Before you take off next time though, why don't you get some more knowledge? I can teach you about engines, and a lot about sailing too."

Skip said, "But I've never even seen you take your boat out of the slip, what do *you* know about sailing?"

Skip meets Mr. Grey

Mr. Grey threw back his head and laughed, "Ha-ha-ha, I don't go sailing *now*…but you've never asked me about my life before, have you? I'm old, my back hurts, and I like taking care of my old wooden boat and staying here in the marina. And besides, I've already sailed all the way around the world. You see Skip, you shouldn't jump to conclusions about people until you get to know them. And if it's wisdom you seek, then you might start hanging out with those who are wise."

Skip's jaw dropped. "You've sailed around the world? Why didn't you tell me?"

"You never asked," laughed Mr. Grey.

Skip looked down apologetically and said, "Gee, you're right, Mr. Grey. I'm sorry. I guess I ignored you because you're older. Will you teach me everything you know? Please, please? I'll be the best student and friend you've ever had, when can we start?!"

"All right Skip, I'll teach you. But you have to promise to work hard and listen carefully to what I tell you, okay?" After Skip promised, Mr. Grey had another question. "Tell me young man, why does a boy like you want to go sailing to Tahiti? Do you really think you'll find your brother? What are you running away from?" Skip explained how the kids at school teased, bullied, and hated him. "I guess I'm running away from all of that, and I really want to find my brother. He's the only family I have left and I'm sure he'd want to be with me."

Skip went on talking rapidly. "Since Mom died, there's nothing for me here anymore. I really want to go, it doesn't feel right for me here. And I just have to find my brother Mr. Grey, please will you help me?"

Mr. Grey objected, "You can't just run away every time you face people who don't like you. Why do you care what they think? They're the dummies and you'll have the last laugh on them." He added, "But I understand about needing to go because I've had that same feeling before. And I must say if I were you, I would want to find my lost brother too." He sat down and thought for a long couple of minutes, then finally waved his hand and simply said, "Let's Go! You're going to have a lot of projects to get the boat ready. There will be provisioning spare parts and food, you'll be learning lots of new knowledge, there will be repairs to make, and lots of things will come up that you never

35

even thought of." The first thing you're going to learn about is making lists. You're going to have lists coming out your ears. So, sit down, stop talking, and start writing. We're going to start with four lists, A,B,C, D. Here's how it works."

"A" is for those things that must be done before going to sea.

"B" is for those things that should be done before going to sea.

"C" is for those things that would be nice to have done before going to sea.

"D" is for don't count on these things getting done before going to sea.

"So let's take a project and see which list it should be on," said Mr. Grey. They discovered the engine problem was a broken water pump. That was an obvious "A" so they could get the engine running again. Varnishing the wood work was a "D" because it wasn't necessary to be done before departure. And so on they went through hundreds of items and divided them among the lists. When they were done, Skip sat back and whistled, then said, "This looks like years worth of projects!"

"I'd say more like a few months or so," said Mr. Grey. "We can do it, there are lots of little things that will go quickly. Let's get started!"

For the next few months, he taught Skip everything he knew about engines, sails, and navigation. They went sailing together, they practiced what to do to secure the boat in storms, took apart and rebuilt pumps, and Skip soaked up the knowledge like a sponge.

One day, Skip announced that he was ready. He couldn't wait any longer and just had to go. "Hold on there a minute," said Mr. Grey. "You can't go yet."

"Why not? What now?" asked a frustrated Skip?

"You haven't given your boat a name. It's bad luck to have a boat with no name. Probably why you had engine trouble right off the bat," said Mr. Grey. "Now go home and take it easy and when you've come up with a name for your boat, come back and we'll give her a proper ceremony."

So Skip went home and thought. And he thought and he thought. He made lists of names such as, "My New Life" "World Explorer" "My Dream" "Adventurer" and fell asleep surrounded by pages of names.

But none of them seemed to be right. He stared at his list for days until it finally occurred to him why he didn't really like any of the names. They were all about him. The more Skip thought about it, the more he realized that the name of his boat should represent something…or someone other than him. That was it! It had to be a person. It had to be someone else. And that person should be the strongest person he has ever known, the one who has inspired him the most, the one who could safeguard him through thick and thin, and who would never let him down.

"Mr. Grey! Mr. Grey!" shouted Skip as he ran down the dock. I have the name! I have the name of my boat!" Skip handed him a piece of paper. As he unfolded it, Mr. Grey looked at it, looked up at Skip, and with a tear rolling down the old man's cheek he said, "Perfect Skip". "That's perfect."

The next day, Skip and Mr. Grey were busy with dark blue paint and stencils. They carefully placed the letters on both sides of the boat, and then painted in the stencils one letter at a time. By the end of the day, they were done and as they peeled off the stencils, you could make out the name one giant blue letter at a time. J—U—L—I—A.

CHAPTER 7—DOES THIS OCEAN EVER END?

Skip was ready this time. He had been studying under Mr. Grey's direction for months and he had absorbed as much of Mr. Grey's unlimited sailing and boating knowledge as his brain could handle. Skip was also learning how to stay calm in tough situations. They had drilled over and over again how to **reef** the sails in a storm to de-power the boat, how to anchor properly, and how to find the boat's position even if the electronics went haywire. Skip's boat had electronic navigation and GPS, but at sea there was no backup, so he had learned to find his position at sea with a **sextant** that measures the position of the sun and stars. It's the same method Cook and Columbus used and Skip was proud to know the old-fashioned method of **celestial navigation**.

The spare parts bins were full, there was extra engine oil, transmission oil, and engine coolant. The water tanks held hundreds of gallons of fresh water, and Skip had stowed enough food to last for two months that now filled every nook and cranny. He expected his first long voyage to last under one month, but he kept hearing his mother say, "Take extra food!"

Was he afraid this time? He sure was. But Mr. Grey had taught Skip how to manage his fears. It was a pretty easy process. First he had to recognize the fear, and admit to himself he was afraid. "Everybody gets afraid," said Mr. Grey. "But most of the time, we're afraid to admit it, as if it's bad to be afraid. But fear is actually a good thing that exists in nature for a reason. How do you think the Antelope outruns the Cheetah? Fear! The Cheetah is running for its dinner but the Antelope is running for its life!" Once he admitted to himself he was afraid, the next step was to accept the fear. He could let the fear in but not let it take control. Mr. Grey explained how fear would provide him with extra strength, kept him sharp, and on his toes. So it turns out that fear wasn't such a bad thing after all. As the days passed at sea, Skip did indeed become more and more comfortable with his fears. His fear made him focused and alert to everything that went on around him. He was learning to live with fear as part of his everyday life.

Day after day, Skip sailed in a southwest direction. The days rolled by like the swells at sea; they kept coming one after another and there seemed no end in sight. Skip wasn't just tired, he was exhausted. He had been sailing by himself across the Pacific Ocean for three weeks and it was hard work sailing JULIA alone. He never imagined the ocean could be this big—where was the end? The water seemed infinite as his boat rode the swells up and down, ever onward, ever southwest toward the island of Tahiti.

The ocean seemed to go on forever

He knew the island wasn't too many more days away but couldn't let his guard down because on a boat, there is no time off or time out. The boat must operate 24 hours a day, 7 days a week and doesn't care if you're tired or not. He kept very busy with the constant effort it took raising, lowering and changing the sails. When sailing through rough conditions he would put up smaller sails, in calm weather, up went the bigger sails. There was never time to just relax as he had to cook his meals, repair broken equipment, forecast the weather (sometimes right, sometimes wrong), and tend to all the daily cleanup chores. Sometimes he was so tired he hallucinated. He saw shapes and images that looked like walls and giant mountains ahead of the boat. One time he slammed the wheel over hard to turn and avoid what he thought was a brick wall in front of the boat. It was only his mind playing tricks on him. The hallucinations were becoming more and more common and he was actually getting used to them. But then the voices started. Nearly every day, he heard his mother speaking to him giving advice as she always had. It was like she was somehow in his head. But Skip didn't believe in ghosts or spirits or anything like that…did he? However, since the boat was named JULIA, and he was hearing his mother's voice, he began to question what he did and did not believe. She seemed to always be there to remind him how strong he could be under the toughest conditions. One time he even heard her give him a good scolding for leaving the milk out of the refrigerator. Skip wondered if he was losing his mind!

Three weeks alone at sea was taking its toll on Skip's mental state. In addition to hearing voices, he had begun talking to himself when things got rough. "C'mon! You can do it, hang in there!" he would say to himself. Was he talking to himself or was he hearing his mother? It didn't really matter because either way, the conversations usually comforted him. Lately he really thought he was going nuts because he had begun talking to the fish and his favorites, the ever-present dolphins. As JULIA plowed through the water creating a wave at the bow, the dolphins would surf on that wave, leaping in and out of the water, looking so relaxed and comfortable. Skip liked to sit at the bow and shout his encouragement, "C'mon dolphins! Jump higher!" and he swore he could see them do just that. It seemed the dolphins never left and that made him happy. One day when there was hardly a breath of wind, and the temperature was so hot the sweat dripped off him like a faucet, Skip heard himself muttering out loud, "Hey Fishy, come here Fishy," as he watched a Mahi Mahi swim near the boat. Was he going nuts in the middle of the Pacific Ocean? Maybe he was, but at least out at sea, there was nobody to tease him, nobody to bully him, and he could do what he wanted when he wanted without anybody calling him names. He didn't care if he ever saw another person again.

Skip was happy: he liked this trip across the ocean, he liked the boat, and he liked being at sea. And while he didn't like how hard he had to work to keep the boat sailing, he thought it was a small price to pay for not having anybody else around to bug him. He reminded himself to trust no one, that everyone was out to ridicule him, and he was destined to be alone so he better learn to like it. He wouldn't mind someone else to talk to but not a human. *Maybe I'll get a parrot, they're very talkative, thought Skip.*

Whack! Skip heard the noise and leaped up out of his bunk, banging his head on the low ceiling above him. "Owww!" He cried, but there was no time to worry about his head. He leaped up the 5-step ladder in one bound and saw the **boom** crashing over to the **port** side. "**Squall!**" shouted Skip, to no one in particular but himself. The sudden strong wind screamed so loud, it sounded like a wounded animal as it howled through the rigging. Looking in all directions, he saw nothing but dark heavy clouds and pouring rain that was hitting him sideways because the wind was so powerful. "Hurry up! Turn downwind! Get the mainsail down! Get the jib furled! Get that forward hatch closed!" Skip was shouting orders left and right to himself. He was learning it was okay to talk to himself, and as he heard the words out loud, he took action. The orders he was shouting over the noise were the same orders Mr. Grey had shouted at him when they had practiced for this. "So this is what Mr. Grey was talking about," muttered Skip as he listened to himself. He was the only one there to take action to save the boat from going wildly out of control in the strong 40-**knot** squall winds. And now, all that counted was action—to protect the boat from being damaged—and to protect himself from getting hurt or falling overboard. "Oh, I wish Mr. Grey was here!"

"Stay calm Skip, don't let the fear of the moment rule. Use your training, remember what you learned," said the calm voice in his head.

Was Mr. Grey in his head? *"Remember why the Antelope outruns the Cheetah, because he is running out of fear for his life."* Or was the training so repetitive that Skip could hear the instructions that were etched into his brain forever? Either way, the training was paying off and Skip knew what to do. He closed all the hatches and then moved quickly forward to the mast so he could bring down the mainsail— always remembering Mr. Grey's words—*"One hand for you, one hand for the boat."* Then he furled the jib, and finally back to the wheel to turn downwind and ride the squall until it blew itself out. He had used a huge amount of energy and was suddenly so exhausted he sat down behind the wheel. He could hear his heart beating so loud, it sounded as if it were going to leap out of his chest. He recognized that sound—it was the sound of fear he had let in—but Skip had taken charge, had used the fear to his advantage, and had tapped into that extra strength fear provides. He remembered Mr. Grey saying, "Skip, fear is just nature's way of making you focus on the task at hand. Don't fight it, use it." The Antelope had outrun the Cheetah.

The good thing about squalls is they don't usually last long and this one was over in 10 minutes. After the violent squall had passed, and he got JULIA back on course, Skip went below and crawled into his bunk, still panting from his sudden burst of adrenalin in his body. He passed out fast asleep almost immediately, but was awakened a few minutes later by the familiar sounds of his friends the dolphins. They were splashing and jumping and it seemed as though they were talking to him. "Eee-eee, eee-eee," and Skip smiled. He listened to the dolphins and to the water rush by as JULIA pounded through the vast ocean toward what he hoped would be white sand beaches, turquoise blue lagoons, swaying palm trees, and a parrot.

Skip awoke to bright sun, calmer seas, and an unusual sound, the squeaking and squealing of birds filled the air as they circled his boat. And that smell? What was that smell? Skip popped his head out the hatch and stared ahead toward the horizon. The clouds in the distance were all clumped in one area and they had a green tint to them. He followed his eyes down and couldn't believe what he saw. "Land!" Skip whispered to himself. "Land! Land-ho!" he shouted. "Land! I smell land!" He shouted for joy and a tear of joy rolled down his cheek. He had never felt more proud in his life. By the end of the day, he would hear the splash of the anchor in the calm lagoon.

CHAPTER 8—SKIP MEETS KANEK

S kip walked alone along the white sandy beach on the island of Tahiti, stopping now and then to admire the wide variety of shells. He never took them from the beach, preferring to appreciate their beauty in their natural surroundings. Rocks were different though, and he couldn't resist skimming the flattest ones across the calm bay. He felt proud of his accomplishment of sailing alone across the Pacific Ocean. He reflected on how just a couple of years earlier, he hadn't even known how to sail, let alone across an entire ocean by himself. He felt strangely alone though. He had emailed Aunt Beatrice to let her know he had arrived and she had replied to be sure and watch out for Polar Bears, as she heard they were dangerous. Skip knew she was a bit nutty, but sheesh! Polar Bears in the South Pacific? She went on to wish him luck because deep down Aunt Beatrice never really wanted Skip in the house anyway. She was lost in her own world and didn't have the time or interest to raise a boy. Mr. Grey had emailed back to help with some of the mechanical problems, and then had lots of questions for Skip including where he was sailing to next. Skip reminded him he was searching for his brother and wouldn't be going anywhere until he found him.

Where would he start his search? Where would he find a young man named Moon Boy on the island of Tahiti? Skip began by drawing a picture of a boy with a crescent moon birthmark on his right leg. He had been showing it to everyone he met but nobody had seen Brian. Maybe he should begin looking for a parrot? Skip skimmed a grey flat stone six times across the clear water. He threw another, then another, and kept throwing until his arm hurt. So he kicked a green coconut down the beach as if it were a soccer ball. He kicked the coconut again, then chased it, kicked it, chased it, kicked it again but this time the coconut flew far to the right, landing in the thick brush away from the water's edge.

"Out of bounds," came a voice from the lush tropical greenery.

Skip shook his head. It must be the heat, he thought as he searched for his coconut-ball in the bushes.

"It was out of bounds," the voice said again. "So it doesn't really matter which coconut you choose."

"Who said that?!" Skip exclaimed.

Skip meets Kanek

"I did," came the voice from high overhead in a palm tree. As Skip looked up, the boy scrambled down the tree with amazing agility, certainly as if he had climbed many palm trees before. He was barefoot and his skin was dark brown, his jet-black hair flopped down to the middle of his neck, he had very big round brown eyes, and seemed to be about Skip's age. He was thin, wore tattered blue shorts with lots of pockets, and a bright yellow t-shirt, and he now stood face to face with Skip. "What are you doing on my beach? You don't look Tahitian, who are you?" He spoke quickly and eagerly, as if he hadn't had a conversation in quite a while.

They introduced themselves and found lots in common. Mainly that each lived alone: Kanek in a makeshift tent on the beach, and Skip on his boat. At first, Kanek couldn't believe that Skip had sailed from California, but when Skip pointed proudly out to the bay where JULIA was anchored. Kanek's jaw dropped. "Wow! That's your boat? From California? By yourself?"

Kanek was all ears as he listened to his new acquaintance's story about sailing across the Pacific by himself and how he was searching for his lost brother. "After my mom died I decided to leave…she actually told me I should go and find Brian…and I think he needs to know about our mom." His voice trailed off softly as he told the story of his mom's instructions to find his brother.

"That's incredible," Kanek said. "I wonder if we're long lost brothers or something. I mean, I've always wanted to go exploring and leave this island…and I don't have any family either." His shoulders drooped and his eyes turned sad as he explained that he was an orphan. His only relative had been his grandfather who lived a long life before the great hurricane claimed him. Kanek lived alone in the wild and had to hide from the authorities who would send him to live with a strange family and Kanek just wasn't cut out for that. He wanted to get off of the island and see what else the world had to offer him, so he had been teaching himself to speak English by talking to tourists and reading English newspapers.

The boys stared at each other in amazement. It did seem as though

50

they were both castaways and were somehow meant to know each other. "I don't suppose you're looking for a crew?" asked Kanek.

Skip was caught off guard by such a forward question after just meeting someone. "I'm looking for my brother," repeated Skip and he showed the drawing of a boy with a crescent shape birthmark to Kanek.

Kanek stood up as he looked at the drawing. "I know of him," Kanek replied almost instantly. He's something of a legend here in Tahiti. They say he came out of nowhere, just showed up and nobody knows where he came from, where he lives, or where he went. His name is Hina, it means Boy of the Moon. Legend is that he always travels in the direction of that crescent moon, as if he was leaving a trail behind him.

Skip looked at Kanek suspiciously. "Nah, you're just yanking my chain aren't you?"

"No, I'm not!" shouted Kanek. "I'm Tahitian and we don't lie. That wouldn't be right and would be an insult to our great heritage. I'm not kidding, I know the legend. My grandfather told it to me and he knew all things about everybody.

"Can we talk to your grandfather?" Skip asked eagerly.

Kanek sat down on the warm white sand. "My grandfather isn't here anymore," Kanek said sadly. "I told you, the great hurricane took him away."

"I'm sorry," said Skip as he plopped down next to Kanek on the beach. "What do you mean that Hina followed the crescent moon?"

"My grandfather explained it like this," and Kanek began drawing in the sand with his finger. "You take a place where you know he was. Then you take a crescent moon shape, upside down like it is on Hina, and always use the same length, that of your fist. You draw the crescent shape over the top of your fist and that's the next place Hina goes to. And by Nami Nami law, he must go that distance every time he makes a move."

"Why does he keep moving," asked Skip?

"He doesn't have to keep moving," replied Kanek. "But when he does move, he has to do so according to Nami Nami law. The rumors say he's a great believer in that and won't vary from it. But..." Kanek's voice trailed off...

"But what?" Skip demanded an answer.

"All I know is the other rumors I heard, so they're not necessarily true."

"What rumors? Tell me!" Skip was starting to raise his voice in aggravation.

"Okay, but remember I'm just repeating what I've heard," Kanek said softly. "They say Hina is a thief, a modern-day pirate. He uses his position of authority and mystery to be taken in by a society, and then steals their riches and moves on."

Skip thought for a moment and said, "My mom said in her letter that he had been in some sort of trouble with the law…you don't suppose…I HAVE TO FIND HIM! I have to save him!"

Kanek sat down and added, "They say he already has a price on his head." Whoever finds him will surely kill him if they find out who he really is and that he's violated Nami Nami law."

"I have to find him first!" Skip mumbled. "Hey Kanek, go back to the crescent shape that you lay down on the chart. What size chart do you use for that? What scale? And what size fist?"

Kanek laughed and said, "You silly, there IS only one chart—that of the great Nami Nami voyagers." There was silence for a few minutes and then Kanek spoke. "You know what I think? I think you need me."

"Huh? Need you for what?" asked Skip.

"I could help you find Hina!" shouted Kanek as he leaped up. "I can be your crew and we can look for Hina together. I know how to find where he went next. Don't you see it? We need to get hold of a Nami Nami map! It also shows the size of the fist to use."

Skip wasn't used to meeting people this easily, and didn't know if he should trust the native boy. Already he was talking about "we" and Skip didn't know what to think. He had never met anyone who didn't tease him or have some pre-disposed opinion of Skip. And he had never met anyone to be so open and honest right away. But friendliness and honesty were indeed part of Tahitian custom and since this was Skip's first experience with another culture, he didn't know quite what to make of it. "Gee, I don't know…I don't even know you. And you don't know how to sail, and you're kind of scrawny. Oh, I'm sorry!" Skip quickly added. "That was mean, that's what everyone does to me when they meet me. They call me chubby and I hate it, and why did I call you a name? I'm really really sorry." Skip sat down on the beach, put his head into his arms and tried his hardest not to cry. "I didn't mean you were weak, but sailing a boat is tough work and I'm not sure you'd be able to handle it. And besides, don't you have other family or friends who are looking for you?"

Kanek looked sad and hurt. "No, I told you, I live alone and have no family. My grandfather taught me all about the winds and the waves and I know how to sail. My grandfather was one of the great Nami Nami who traveled in huge dugout sailing canoes from island to island. He even journeyed from Tahiti to New Zealand and back. I miss him and his stories a lot. When he got really excited, which he did a lot, his right eye would start to twitch and just that one eye would blink really fast. It was almost as if just his eye were talking. And he taught me to be tough too—I may look scrawny, but I'm stronger than I look and I'm quick too—you want to wrestle?! C'mon!" With that, Kanek jumped onto Skip, spun him around onto his back and pinned him to the ground in no time. "There, you still think I'm scrawny?" laughed Kanek. But he meant it. He was a tough kid and he wanted to be sure Skip knew that.

"Okay Okay, I give!" shouted Skip. "But really? You mean to tell me you don't answer to anybody? You're totally free to do whatever you want any time?" Skip asked.

Kanek nodded. "In fact, if I don't get off of this island, someone is going to find me living alone and put me into a foster home and I can't live like that."

Skip thought about the long ocean passage he had just completed and while he was proud of himself, it had been really difficult alone. Then he thought about a parrot as company and realized that Kanek was a much better choice. "Well, okay, but it's only for a trial period to see how you do. If you can't pull your own weight, you're off the boat, okay?" Skip had straightened up to look more captain-like. As they stood facing each other, Kanek nodded and grinned while he brought his right hand up to a salute. "Aye aye Skipper," he said as he stuck out his hand. They shook hands to their new friendship and Skip said, "C'mon, I'll show you the boat. Let's Go!" The two boys raced down the beach, Kanek far ahead of Skip who still couldn't run very fast in spite of losing some of his belly fat after spending so much time at sea. They hopped into the dinghy and rowed out to where JULIA lay at anchor. Neither boy ever looked back.

CHAPTER 9—THE SEARCH BEGINS

The boys spent the next two days sneaking in and out of a few villages in Tahiti as they tried to find a Nami Nami map of the pacific ocean islands. Finally late on the second night, Kanek had spotted a real Nami Nami map next to the sleeping mat of one of the village chief's sons. Kanek had quietly snuck up to the map, reached his hand out and was just about to grab it, when suddenly a large bare hand slammed down on his skinny wrist pinning Kanek to the ground.

"Hoi-a, what are you doing here, demanded the chief's son?!

"Shhh!" Kanek put his finger up to his lips. "Please, I need this Nami Nami map. My friend and I are looking for Hina, Boy of the Moon, the traveler with the mark of the crescent. We need the Nami Nami map to know where he went. My friend is his brother!"

"I know who Hina is," said the chief's son as he eased his foot off of Kanek's wrist.

"I can pay you for the map," said Kanek.

"You know I can't accept money for a Nami Nami map. The Nami Nami maps may be rare and hard to find, but they must go to where they are needed. If you are voyaging across the ocean and need the map, then tradition says I must give it to you. Take it. Go and make the Nami Nami proud," said the chief's son.

It was late and very dark when Kanek finally returned to the beach where he had left Skip. "I got it! I got it!" he whispered loudly. They hopped into the dinghy, rowed out to JULIA, and climbed aboard. As they spread the old Nami Nami map out on the chart table down below, they looked it over with eyes wide open taking in every little detail the map had to offer. It was as if they were looking at an old treasure map. It had ocean currents, wind directions, island locations, and in the lower right corner was an upside down crescent shaped moon.

"How do we know how big a fist is?" asked Skip. Our hands are smaller than grownups. They looked closely at the map and tried to figure out how to measure a fist size when Kanek spotted it.

"Look Skip! Here!" Kanek was looking in the lower left corner of the map. "See this drawing of four coconut trees? They make what looks like a circle. But see how the palm fronds are indented, like the knuckles on a hand? See, when I put my hand down in a fist, it looks the same, except mine is smaller. That's gotta be it, that's the length of a fist. So that's the distance we use for a crescent shape from Tahiti. But in which direction?"

"West," said Skip. He had to go west. It's the way of the wind and currents. Nobody in their right mind would try to head against the wind and current direction."

"That of course assumes Hina is in his right mind," added Kanek. "So let's say he did go west, let's map it out and see where it puts us." The boys got busy making a crescent shaped piece of paper the size of the fist drawn on the map. They placed one end of the crescent on Tahiti and moved the other end around in a westerly direction. The crescent spanned over the Cook Islands, Tonga, Fiji, and landed on just one place; the islands of Vanuatu. But which island in the chain? There were more than 80 islands.

"We have to get more precise," said Skip. We have to know which island in Vanuatu. Skip began searching through a drawer filled with papers. After a couple of minutes of looking, he pulled out a post card. It was the last post card his brother Brian (Hina) had sent from Tahiti. Skip examined it very closely, turning it over to look at the picture, then the writing, and then back to the picture. Finally, his eyes lit up. "Look Kanek! Look at the picture of the mountain on your island of Tahiti. That volcano has been quiet for a long time, right?"

"Yeah, my grandfather said it last erupted thousands of years ago."

"Then why did Brian draw smoke coming out of the top of it," asked Skip?

"I don't know, maybe he likes volcanos?" offered Kanek.

"Kanek, help me make a more precise crescent measure. I think I know where Brian is." Together they perfected the size and shape of a new measuring piece of paper, then set it down on the map with one point resting precisely on Tahiti. They rotated the other end around the map to the west and sure enough, it landed right onto only one island; Tanna. "That's it! He has to be on Tanna, home of one of the world's most active volcanoes. I just know he's on Tanna!" Upon further investigation though, they found it to be the same distance to New Zealand.

"How do we know he didn't go to New Zealand?" asked Kanek.

"Because of the picture Kanek," said Skip. Hina drew smoke and steam coming out of the top of a volcano. Don't you think that means he was looking for a live volcano? One that is erupting daily?" Kanek nodded in agreement. "Problem is, Vanuatu is…according to my calculations…about 2,700 miles away, that's about 18 days of nonstop sailing or a couple of months if we stop along the way."

Kanek whistled. "That's a long sail Skip. Are we up for it?"

"If you don't want to go, that's okay," said Skip. "I can go back to my original plan and get a parrot."

"Oh yeah, well I can go back to my plan of, of, of…" His voice trailed off because Kanek didn't have another plan. "Hey Skip, I have a better idea. Why don't WE get a parrot and all three of us sail for Vanuatu!"

Skip mumbled, "Now, where to get a parrot…."

"I know where to find a parrot!" shouted Kanek. "Mango lives in the same tree I was in when we met! He's awesome!" Within a few days, the boys had provisions onboard and the three crew of JULIA were ready to sail. There were three because they now counted Mango the parrot as part of the crew. Mango was friendly and very talkative and repeated what he heard without too much encouragement needed. His bright orange and yellow feathers had accents of white and grey showing he wasn't a newborn. He was one more gift from the village chief's son who gave the boys the Nami Nami map. As the boys loaded food onboard, Mango kept saying, "Mango likes cookies, Mango likes cookies," until they fed him a cookie. Then he would just bob his head up and down and watch from his perch.

As JULIA sailed away from Tahiti, Kanek turned to look back at what used to be his home. He turned to Skip with a sad look on his face and said, "I guess now we're both adrift with no home."

"We have a home Kanek, we're on it right now. But if you don't go forward and help get that jib to set right, I might just have to leave you behind!"

"Aye, Skipper!" said Kanek as he moved easily forward on the boat.

Instead of stopping along the way, the boys had decided to push hard and sail straight through to the island of Tanna where they hoped to catch up to Brian, or Hina as they now called him. Since they had never sailed together, it was going to be a long three weeks as they learned to understand and anticipate each other's looks, comments, and silences. As the days progressed, the boys seemed to get along well. Kanek was, as expected, open with his feelings and trusting of his new friend. Skip was wary of this easiness, and seemed to always be looking for a reason to pick on Kanek. One night while Skip was off watch, he was lying in his bunk reading about Kodo dragons as he liked to do. He heard loud noises coming from the foredeck so he poked his head out the hatch into the cockpit. Kanek was nowhere to be seen. "Kanek? Kanek! Kanek!!!" Skip leaped out of his bunk and raced up to the cockpit looking around.

"Oh, hey Skip, what are you doing up?" came a voice from the foredeck.

"What are you doing up there Kanek?" Skip screamed in a shrill voice.

"That same jib sheet keeps getting tangled so I came forward to re-lead it. I don't think it will tangle anymore," said Kanek in a cheery voice.

Skip could barely control his temper and then he just burst out loud. "Kanek, where's your safety harness?! How many times have I told you that when you're up here by yourself, you have to wear your safety harness?"

"I know, I know," Kanek said apologetically. But Skip couldn't let it go. This was the third time this had happened, and at the speed they were going, and especially at night, all it would take is one unexpected wave to plop the unsuspecting crew overboard. And it would be impossible to go back and find him. Skip had let it go with a simple caution the previous times as he didn't want to get too angry over what Kanek had called 'such a small thing.'

This time was different as Skip seemed to explode any and all anger he had about everything that had gone wrong in his life. He shouted and yelled, stomped and stamped his feet, shook and pounded his fists, and was turning red from all of the frustration that boiled up inside.

"Take it easy Skip, okay, okay, I'll wear my harness. Sheesh! It's not that big of a deal."

Mango was down below bobbing his head and dancing back and forth on his perch repeating, "Wear your harness, wear your harness!"

"It is to me!" Skip shouted back at him. "It is to me." He went below and wouldn't talk to Kanek for an entire day after that. He was seething with anger.

On the second day after their argument, Kanek gingerly approached Skip and asked quietly, "I guess you'll be wanting me to get off the boat as soon as we get to Tanna? That's okay. I just want you to know that I'm really sorry and I've been wearing my harness every night." Kanek's big brown eyes showed his fear. After what seemed like an eternity to Kanek, Skip slowly raised his gaze and Kanek could see tears running down his cheeks. "Skip? What's the matter Skip? Why are you crying?"

"Don't you get it Kanek? I don't want you to get off the boat. That's not why I was yelling at you. I truly don't want you to get off the boat and especially not at sea at night. I don't want to lose you. I'm scared of losing you. You're all I have Kanek. I want you to wear your harness so you stay safe, okay?" Kanek was speechless. His mouth opened but no words came out. He just walked over to Skip and gave him a big Tahitian hug. "Now get out of here, aren't you supposed to be on watch?" Skip said with a smile. Kanek nearly danced his way back to the cockpit.

"Wear your harness, wear your harness, wear your harness!"

"I am wearing my harness" shouted Kanek.

"That wasn't me," Skip shouted back. "It was Mango!" That broke the ice and the boys enjoyed a much needed laugh.

After 19 days at sea, Skip was feeling very lucky they hadn't had any really bad weather. Sure, there was the occasional squall, but for the most part the Pacific Ocean lived up to its translation of "peaceful." On the morning of the 19th day, Skip was sitting at the chart table below decks tapping his pencil on the navigation chart thinking, *I don't understand it, we should be looking at land by now.* He knew they had run into some light winds that had slowed them down, but it couldn't have been more than a half day delay….

And sure enough, as if he had willed it to be, Skip heard the shout from above, "Land Ho! Skip! Land Ho!" Skip raced up to the cockpit to see Kanek dancing around with the binoculars in one hand and the wheel in the other. "Woo-hoo! Land!" He handed Skip the binoculars so he could see for himself. Skip took one look through them, then looked back at Kanek and smiled. They had done it. They had covered 2700 miles averaging 150 miles a day and they were still in one piece!

"Land Ho! Land Ho! Land Ho!" came the cry from down below as Mango was jumping around the cabin shouting with excitement.

Vanuatu is one of the most out-of-the-way island countries in the world. Located in a remote part of the South Pacific, its more than 80 islands are covered in lush greenery dotted with stark black and grey land, clearly showing these islands were created by volcanic eruptions millions of years ago. But unlike most volcanic areas of the world, in Vanuatu the volcanoes are still active. On the island of Tanna; dark ash and smoke can be seen discharging into the sky from the top of the Yasur Volcano. It was an eerie looking sight for Skip and Kanek; it seemed like the whole island was exploding.

Rather than race to shore and look for Hina, the boys felt they needed a well-deserved rest of a few days. They were in a perfect place for it too. Not more than a hundred yards away from JULIA's anchorage was a hissing steam vent heating the sea water at the edge of the bay to over 100 degrees. The small pools created by the black lava rock formations at the shore made a perfect natural hot tub surrounded by ten-foot tall green ferns and lush jungle vines, and Skip and Kanek swam over to the pools for a relaxing soak in the hot salt water. Unlike the turquoise color of the ocean in Tahiti, these waters were a deep dark blue reflecting the black sand bottom, only adding to the mysterious feeling of these islands.

The next day, Skip and Kanek decided to try to catch some lobsters. They had watched the native boys catching big lobsters with their bare hands so they decided to try their luck. Skip was hesitant, but Kanek urged him to try. "All they can do is bite!" Kanek laughed. He was clearly very comfortable in this endeavor—much more so than Skip. They donned their masks and fins and swam over to where the natives were, exchanged friendly "Hello's," and asked permission to also try for lobster. After catching their breath, Skip and Kanek each took a big gulp of air, aimed their feet at the sky, and dove straight down under water with the rock wall right in front of them. Skip was only under water for about ten seconds before he had to pop to the surface gasping for air, but Kanek was at home down there. He popped to the surface about thirty seconds later, gulped some more air and immediately went back down under water. Skip didn't have the stamina for another dive so he just watched in awe as Kanek slipped his hand between two cracks in the rock wall, grabbed a foot-long lobster and popped to the surface! "Here you go Captain," as he handed the squirming lobster to Skip. Kanek had clearly done this many times before and was was enjoying impressing Skip with his native skills. Skip was indeed surprised, especially when Kanek came to the surface with a second lobster! Skip and the natives cheered as they admired their catch of two huge lobsters.

"Where did you learn to do that?" asked Skip. "Never mind, that's a dumb question isn't it. You're from Tahiti! Well done! Can you get more?" Skip was clearly impressed and Kanek felt he had made a little headway toward earning Skip's trust.

"I could get more, but I won't," answered Kanek. "We got two and there are two of us. That's more than enough and we only take what we can eat. Now, how are we going to cook these things, they're giant!" asked Kanek. One of the local boys motioned for them to follow, and together they all swam over to the natural hot pools. A boy named Peter showed Kanek which pool was the hottest and after making sure the net bag was tied tight, they dropped the lobsters into the hot pool as if they were in a big pot boiling on the stove! When the lobsters were finished boiling, Kanek pulled one of them out of the net bag and handed it to

Peter who was touched by the gesture. The local kids were about the same age as Skip and Kanek and they all got along well. The locals were friendly, eager to help, and proved to be excellent tour guides, but none had heard of Hina. Together they explored the island, brought Skip and Kanek to their village, and provided them with fresh fruit every day. They had English names such as Henry, Peter, Richard, and John because Vanuatu used to be under England's control. And while they didn't ask for anything, they truly appreciated all of the gifts that Skip and Kanek showered upon them. They were in need of batteries, t-shirts, swimming goggles, rope, fishing hooks, and were amazed at how much stuff was aboard JULIA. And while it seemed as though these native kids had so little in the way of material possessions, they were happy every day. It made Skip and Kanek think. Skip asked, "How can they be so happy when they don't even have a t-shirt without holes in it?"

Kanek said, "I know why. My grandfather always told me that we should appreciate what we have, without always wanting something else and something new." Skip was soon to learn this was the way of the islands. Some of the happiest people he met had the fewest possessions.

The next afternoon, as Skip and Kanek hiked along the narrow jungle path toward the volcano, they got an eerie sense. It felt similar to when they saw the movie Jurassic Park, except this was the real thing. The overgrown jungle was one thing, but it was the noises that put them on edge. Odd-looking birds in all colors called from overhead, monkeys screeched as they bounded from tree to tree, giant dragonflies more than a foot long buzzed around their heads, and mosquitoes bit away at their exposed skin. As they walked further inland, the jungle became thicker and darker and they felt like a Raptor was going to leap out and devour them in one gulp!

In a flash, Skip started running ahead and shouted back over his shoulder, "C'mon Kanek! I can see it!" Their hearts were beating fast as they ran forward on the path, jumping over fallen trees, pushing aside the jungle branches, and in less than a minute, they popped out into the bright sunshine.

What lay before them was a sight neither had expected. From the dark green jungle, they emerged onto what looked like the moon. Their feet sunk into the dark grey powdery ash and that was all they could see in every direction. Directly in front of them loomed the huge mysterious crater the local island boys had talked about many times. Steam and smoke rose from its top and they heard a loud hissing sound like escaping gas, and then a more throaty, deep-sounding roar like a blowtorch or flamethrower.

Stepping slowly and ever so lightly, Skip and Kanek made their way up the steep trail that traced back and forth across the mountainside. Their anticipation mounted and they started to realize what a dangerous position they were in because the trail was scattered with still smoldering hot lava rocks, which had recently been flung from inside the crater. There were no barriers to keep them away and no park ranger to tell them to get back behind the fence—there was no fence—this was the real thing! Instead of watching their step on the trail, they found themselves forced to keep their eyes on the sky because lava chunks were landing near them! "Look out!" shouted Kanek as he jumped to the side of the track more than once.

At the top of the trail, Skip and Kanek stopped to catch their breath, looked up, and nearly fell over backwards from the sight. They were standing on the edge of a real, live, active volcano that easily measured a half-mile across. It was enormous. Speechless, they gawked at the huge sunken crater's center where smoke spewed from a red molten pit hundreds of yards wide. Out of this pit flew pieces of lava so red hot they still glowed and smoked after landing on the ground, some not more than fifty feet from where they stood.

Standing on the edge of the volcano

The boys soon noticed that some of the pieces of rock being shot out of the crater were the size of small cars and were soaring hundreds of feet into the air. How much pressure inside the earth did it take to do that?! They sat and watched the eruptions for hours and as the day turned to night, the colors of the smoke changed from white to yellow, and finally to a deep red reflecting the molten fire pit below. Every few minutes, their feet and legs trembled as the ground began a deep low rumble, then a roar, followed by another even bigger eruption shooting more huge lava rocks high into the air. At first the show seemed magical, then mysterious, and then almost evil as the sky glowed bright red and orange as if it was the devil's breath. As they looked into the crater, they saw flames erupting and Skip thought he heard laughter. It was easy to see how the islanders spoke of magical spirits in the depths of the volcano. Were there really spirits in there? Were they good or evil? Was it magic? Why was this part of the earth still on fire? They had so many questions and the boys vowed to learn more about volcanoes. They slowly made their way in silence down the ashen slopes eager to get back to the boat. The volcano seemed to be getting more active as the afternoon wore on, and they were tired from their long day. "Hurry up Skip, there are lots of hot rocks flying around, let's get out of here." But Skip wasn't paying attention, he was lost in his own world of thoughts.

Suddenly, the silence was broken. "Skip! Look out!" shouted Kanek who was watching what looked like a ton of hot rocks the size of golf balls headed right for them. But it was too late when Skip looked up— one of the rocks was headed right for him. In a flash, Kanek leaped with all his might at Skip, pushing him to the ground making the lava rock miss hitting him square in the head, but skimming his ear. Skip sat up holding his left ear which was burned and bright red. "Are you all right Skip? You have to be more careful."

Skip looked at Kanek and said, "Owwwwwww! My ear is on fire!"

"No it's not, you'll be okay, but let's get you back to the boat and put something on that. Your ear looks like that cooked lobster we had yesterday!"

Back at the boat, after letting Kanek put some burn salve on his ear Skip said, "Kanek, you might have just saved my life. Thank you. And oh, by the way, your trial period is over!" It wasn't easy for Skip, but maybe he was learning to let go of his distrust of people just a little bit at a time.

"We've asked everybody if they know about Hina and come up with nothing," Skip said to Kanek and their new friend Peter.

"Not everybody," Peter said thoughtfully. "There's one man who knows everybody and everything, my Uncle Yans. He only comes out of the bush once a week. What day is it?"

"Friday," said Skip much to the delight of Peter.

"Lucky you then," said Peter. "Because he only visits the village here on the water on Saturdays. Tomorrow we shall seek him out and ask about Hina. I'm not sure if he'll meet with you though, he only meets with people he feels are deserving of his wisdom. I'll see what I can do."

The boys could hardly sleep from their excitement about meeting with Yans, the man who knew everybody and everything. They were up bright and early, rowed the dinghy ashore to meet up with Peter, and together they set off for the village. By the time they got there, it was mid-morning and already the sweat was dripping off of the boys from the heat and humidity. "You guys wait here," Peter said as he turned to go into the village. It's customary for strangers to stand at the edge of the village and await an invitation to enter. The boys stood awkwardly in the sun as the villagers looked at them with great curiosity. Finally, after what seemed like an eternity, Peter came running back and with a broad beaming smile announced, "Yans is here! I told him how kind you have been and how generous you are with giving. He has invited us to lunch in the hut of the village chief!" Kanek knew instinctively this was a great honor and began explaining to Skip that he should be humble, gentle, and very respectful of both the chief and Yans. He went on to describe how important the elders were in a village and how their great wisdom was accepted as the rule of law.

After the boys shared a meal of taro, bananas, and fried fish with the village elders, Skip nudged Peter to ask about Hina. "Let me do the talking," said Peter and he began telling Skip's story. He explained to the chief and Yans how Skip was searching for his lost brother, known in Tahiti as Boy of the Moon because of the crescent moon birthmark. He drew the upside down crescent in the sand and immediately the chief and Yans began chattering so fast in a native language, Peter barely understood. He asked politely if they could explain their excitement and they laughed as Yans slowly explained. It was only a few months ago they had seen Hina on their island. He had arrived on a steamer delivering supplies from Tahiti.

"Do you know what that means?" Kanek jumped in. "It means that our measurement of distance and direction of the crescent moon was correct! We got it right!"

"But where is he now?" asked Skip. Peter interpreted for Yans and the chief. Both laughed and shrugged their shoulders.

Then Yans spoke in broken English. "Hina follow crescent moon, leave trail, I show." He got up and waved for the boys to follow him as they walked to a tiny beach cove of tall black rock cliffs covered in huge ferns. Yans pointed up the steep cliff to what looked like an indentation in the rock wall. It was probably 100 feet up from where they stood. "Hina live there," Yans said. He then bowed to the boys, said a ritual chant of good luck, turned, and walked away leaving the Peter, Skip, and Kanek staring at the cliff.

"It must be the entrance to a cave," said Peter. "There are caves all through these cliffs, but that one doesn't look very easy to get to." The boys sat down on the sand and pondered the idea of scaling a 100 foot cliff to see if Hina left a clue in the cave.

"If Brian could get up there, then why can't we?" said Skip with a puzzled face.

Kanek offered, "I could scramble up there, I'm sure of it!" but Skip wouldn't allow it due to the obvious danger.

"Hey Peter, can you show us how to get to the top of the cliff? Maybe there's a way down from the top," said Skip trying to think his way through the problem.

"Sure, no problem, follow me," as Peter led the boys on a winding trail through thick jungle growth up the backside of the cliff. After half an hour, they were standing at the top of the cliff looking down. "Doesn't look much better from up here!" Peter said as he backed away from the cliff's edge.

The boys were wandering around the top of the cliff looking for any clues to how to enter Hina's cave. The ground was black lava covered in thick green growth and just as Skip was about to call it quits, he heard a shout, "Aaaaarrrrrggghhh!" and then a splash of water. "Skip! Help! Help!" Both Peter and Skip looked around for Kanek but he was gone! "Help! Skip! Peter!" Help!" The boys rushed to where they heard the voice and pushed the greenery away. There in front of them was a hole in the black rock about two feet wide. Skip peeked down into the chasm and saw Kanek about 10 feet below them standing in knee deep water. "I'm okay, and I think I found the way in!" shouted Kanek. "I can see the light at the end of the cave from here!"

"Kanek, how are you going to get out?" asked Skip, but within a minute he had his answer. Kanek's head popped out of the hole in the ground with a big ear to ear grin. "Easy, just take the stairs!" laughed Kanek. "Look, there are cutouts in the rock for hand and footholds and you can climb straight up or down into the cave. "Come on!"

Skip and Peter eased their way down into the hole in the lava, found the carved places for hands and feet, and slowly worked their way down to the pool of shallow water where Kanek was waiting for them. And sure enough, there was the light showing the entrance to the cave on the cliff face. The boys slowly made their way toward the light and stopped at the entrance, the three of them just staring at the 100 foot drop below them. As they turned around, Kanek spotted it first. "Look guys!" There, right in front of them was a map carved into the lava rock wall. "It's a NamiNami map! Skip look, it has the upside down crescent moon carved onto it. One tip is here and the other looks like a tiny island. Looks like a word, can you make it out?"

Skip had been studying the charts and knew most of the islands within the crescent moon distance. "I don't believe it," said Skip. I know what it says. He took a deep breath and let out one word, "Kodo."

A cold wind blew through the cave and several bats took flight making the boys shudder with chills. "What's Kodo?" asked Kanek innocently. "Wait, you don't mean Kodo as in Kodo Dragons, do you?!"

Skip knew and so did Peter and they just said, "C'mon, let's get out of here and go back to the boat."

"What's Kodo?" asked Kanek again. "And what's the rest of it say? Looks like Y and then some scratches in the rock."

"I'll tell you later, c'mon let's get out of here. All that matters is that it says Kodo!" They hastily climbed back up out of the cave and hiked their way back to the beach where the dinghy sat waiting. The three boys jumped in and rowed out to JULIA, climbed aboard and sat huddled together as Skip explained to Kanek and Peter what he knew about Kodo.

CHAPTER 10—THE WORST PASSAGE EVER—AND THE BEST

It was time to go. Cyclone season was fast approaching which meant huge storms could hit Vanuatu during that time of year. While learning about these seasons, Skip discovered that cyclones, typhoons, and hurricanes are all the same enormous type of storm, but are named differently depending on where in the world the storm is located. In Vanuatu, which was in the South Pacific, the storms were called Cyclones and the best way to get out of their usual path was to sail south to Australia. While finding Hina was their first priority, they had to always consider the weather. Their next destination was the mysterious island of Kodo, but it was the wrong season to go there and to do so would be asking for trouble from the weather. Skip was actually feeling guilty for not pressing on to Kodo immediately, but the reputation of cyclones in the area was so bad, Kanek had brought him to his senses. So they decided to head for Australia first, then up to Kodo in Indonesia. Even thought they were sad to leave Peter and their other new-found friends on Vanuatu, the boys were excited—each for their own reasons. Australia! Kangaroos, surfing (Yay!), crocodiles (Boo), more warm days on the beach, and civilization! While Skip loved the

71

excitement of exploring remote places, he hadn't forgotten about super-markets, hardware stores, and the wide variety of foods he had been used to at home. He was discovering he was happiest with a balanced life—remote exploration is great, but so are stores filled with goods to satisfy every personal or nautical need or want. Kanek had never seen the big stores and choices of food Skip had described and boy oh boy, he was excited to experience it all for the first time!

From Vanuatu, it's 1150 miles southwest across the Coral Sea to the huge continent of Australia. The boys expected an 8-day passage and were excited and confident as JULIA sailed away from Vanuatu and headed for blue water. They had planned their "watch-schedule," which determined what time each of them would be on watch sailing, or off watch to cook and sleep. With only two on board, they opted for 3-hour watches. Three hours on, three hours off and this went on 24 hours a day, every day, because life aboard a boat at sea never sleeps. Everything onboard seemed to be just fine and all systems check out okay. But on a boat, looks can be deceiving and you never know what's going to happen next. There was no way Skip and Kanek could predict how many things were about to go wrong.

That first afternoon, as they hoisted the big round red, white, and blue spinnaker, they heard a sickening sound that gave them the chills, "Rrrrrriiiiiiippp!" As they watched in disbelief, the boys witnessed their beautiful sail tear right up the middle for its entire length. "Ohhhh noooo," said Kanek. Together they struggled to lower the shredded sail, stowed it away, hoisted another smaller sail, and continued on. Skip muttered, "That's a bad way to start a passage."

That night, Skip couldn't shake the feeling that perhaps they had brought along an angry spirit from the volcano, because at about midnight, Kanek woke him up with a very loud yell, "Hey Skipper, you better get up here!" Skip jumped out of his bunk and flew up to the cockpit where he found Kanek wrestling with the steering wheel. "The wind just came up suddenly!" shouted Kanek. Indeed it had as Skip saw the wind speed hit 40 knots and the seas increasing in size. At first, Skip thought it was a squall that would end in 10 minutes so he told Kanek to turn the boat to go with the direction of the wind and while it was a fast ride, they got the situation under control. Then Skip went back down below to the navigation station where the radios were located and tuned in the weather broadcast. What he heard gave him the chills. They were forecasting much more than a squall—this was a true South Pacific storm.

"How could I be so stupid?!" Skip shouted to no one in particular. "How did I miss this forecast for such a big storm? When will I ever be good at anything I do? I can't even listen to the radio without screwing it up! Hey, what about *you*, didn't *you* hear the weather forecast before we departed? What good is it having you aboard?!" he shouted directly at Kanek.

"Me? You never said I should be listening to the radio," Kanek retorted. "You said you were the one in charge of weather forecasts."

"Well you should have listened too," Skip lashed out with anger. "Now look at the fix we're in!"

"Maybe I shouldn't be here then because it's not my fault," Kanek said now very defensively. "If you had told me to I would have, but you said we each had our jobs. Remember, I was stowing away the food and provisions. Besides, I thought you said you knew what to do in a storm? You said that friend of yours, Mr. What's-his-name taught you."

Kanek was right. Mr. Grey had taught him what to do during a storm and he had gone through that squall when crossing the big Pacific Ocean by himself and he had come out of it alive. "What are we doing standing down here?" Skip said in a hurry. "Let's go!"

Skip and Kanek went back up to the cockpit and got to work. While Skip had practiced preparing for storms with Mr. Grey, this was his first real storm that would test his training. He knew what to do, but doing those tasks on a pitching and heaving boat was easier said than done. They had to get the big jib down, put a smaller storm jib up, and reef, or reduce the size of the mainsail. They knew how to reef but the process isn't exactly easy—especially in 40-knot winds and seas that had now built to 12-feet tall. But regardless of the conditions, it was still the same step-by-step process every time. While Skip steered through the rough seas, Kanek had to go to the mast and lower the sail down, tie it off at its new size and then tighten it up. And he had to do this while being hooked onto the boat with his 3-foot tether…kind of like a leash so he wouldn't be flung overboard. It was exhausting work and by the time they were through, they both collapsed into the cockpit tired as dogs.

Having smaller sails was like easing up on a car's gas pedal and it made the boat much more manageable. After a few minutes rest, Skip gave Kanek a high-five and said, "Way to go, you did a great job up there. And hey Kanek,"….Skip had a hard time saying the words but eventually got it out. "I'm sorry for yelling at you earlier. You're right, the weather forecast was my job, and I screwed that up. And Kanek, I'm glad you're here." They smiled at each other, still panting from the hard work, and slapped a high-five.

While the next two days were trouble free, it was still a rough ride. The winds never let up to less than 30 knots, and the seas never dropped to smaller than 8 feet high. It was exhausting sailing, but they kept themselves motivated by talking about happy things like the surfing they would soon be doing on the beaches of Australia.

On the fourth day, the storm took on new energy and the winds hit 45 knots, then 50, 55, and the last time they looked at the **anemometer**, it read over 60 knots! That's just over 69 miles per hour, faster than freeway driving! The seas were coming from the port side and made the boat roll steeply to starboard as each wave swooshed under it. JULIA lurched forward with a burst of speed, then slowed, and rolled back to port as if she were getting ready for the next wave. The whole process then started all over again. At nightfall, the rain began coming down in buckets and when combined with that much wind, came at them sideways and stung the boys' faces. The seas came crashing over the side of the boat and the only way they could tell if they were being drenched by rain or sea was the taste of saltwater on their lips. They were in it now! Cooking was nearly impossible and they were eating peanut butter on crackers, and cold beans and chili out of cans. The smell of the opened food cans combined with the rough seas made their stomachs churn and more than once, they each had **tossed their cookies** overboard. Mango hid inside a clothes locker tucked in behind sweaters and jackets. Strangely, she didn't utter a word, and would only eat crackers.

On they sailed towards Australia. Skip wore his bright yellow foul weather gear, tethered into the cockpit, holding onto the wheel like the reins of a bucking bronco horse as JULIA charged into the night. They sailed on that way for another whole day with Kanek relieving Skip at the **helm** for his watch.

CHAPTER 10 – THE WORST PASSAGE EVER – AND THE BEST

The next night convinced the boys they had indeed brought along an angry spirit from the volcano. It was about 2 in the morning, the wind was still howling, the boat was still rolling, and the rain was still coming sideways. All of a sudden, they heard what sounded like a gunshot, "Bang!"

"What the heck was that?!" they said to each other. Kanek got the big powerful flashlight and began searching all over the boat and in a minute he saw it. "The **forestay** is gone!" The forestay is key in holding the mast upright. Before either of them could say another word, they watched in horror as the huge 60-foot tall aluminum mast creaked, groaned, cracked and finally broke in half midway up. The top half teetered for a few seconds, then came crashing down with a loud "Clang, bang, boom," bouncing twice on the fiberglass deck and then splashing loudly as it hit the water. Still connected by the other cables, lines, and with the sails still attached, the whole mess came to a rest as it lay sideways across the deck. No longer powered by her sails, JULIA stopped in the heavy seas and began rolling steeply from side-to-side.

Skip and Kanek stared dumbfounded at the tangled mess. Kanek started to shake and shiver as if he were going into shock and blurted out, "Are we going to sink? Should we launch the life raft? Skip, I'm scared!" Kanek could barely get the words out of his quivering lips. Skip was frozen in his tracks and stared at Kanek, at the tangled mess, and then back at Kanek. JULIA was being thrown around in the rough seas and for a long minute, the boys stood, not knowing what to do first. Skip's thoughts slipped out loud, "This is it, I don't know what to do," and he too started shaking uncontrollably.

Everything goes wrong on the worst passage ever

"Eee-eee! Eee-eee!" Suddenly, there were dolphins everywhere. They were circling the boat, some were jumping, some were screaming, and one huge dolphin kept standing up on its tail screeching loudly, "Eee-eee! Eee-eee!" Just then, Skip thought he heard a faint voice in the distance. It sounded so familiar, but he thought he was hallucinating again. It was coming from inside his head and he recognized the voice—it was Mom! Was it real? No, this was in his head! Wasn't it? *"Skip, don't be afraid, you're strong, you know what to do, you know how to deal with this. Remember you must persevere, you must stay focused on saving the boat, you must keep a positive attitude, and you boys must work together. I know you can do this and you know it too. My name's on that boat so don't you let her sink! Now get to work, and know I'm watching over you...."*

Skip didn't know how to react to the voice in his head, but they snapped him to life. With a new energy, he looked Kanek squarely in the eye, grabbed him by the shoulders and shouted right into Kanek's face, "Kanek! We are NOT going to sink! Do you understand me?! I know you're afraid, I am too, but we're going to be okay, I just know it. So we're scared. Don't think about the fear. There's not much we can do about it, so let's get to work, okay?" Kanek just stared at him with a blank look on his face. "Kanek, listen to me! I need you to listen! We can make it. We're only 350 miles from Australia. Heck, we can make that!" Skip wasn't sure where that little speech had come from or what had just happened inside of him, but all of a sudden he was no longer Skip—he was captain. He was the leader and the last thing he needed was a crew frozen with fear. He needed a crew who was confident and it was his job to inspire that confidence.

Based on everything he had ever read, and Mr. Grey's stories of being at sea , Skip proceeded to make up a plan on the spot. "Kanek, here's what we're going to do," and Skip laid out a plan for cutting the top half of the mast free and using the lower half to carry a very small mainsail they had aboard that was made for extremely heavy winds. "We're going to need the heavy wire cutters," said Skip, "And the biggest hammer we have. Can you find those and bring them up here and fast!" Kanek still didn't speak but turned and headed below to get the tools.

The boys worked feverishly together. It was dark, wet, and cold, and the only light was from their headlamps as they shone through the heavy rain. Both boys were clipped onto the boat with their short **tethers** so they wouldn't fall overboard. It was hard work cutting cables and wires, and pounding with the big hammer to break the rig free from the boat. Hour after hour they kept at it while trying to save what they could for their soon to be created shorter mast.

As the dark night slowly gave way to morning light, the wind eased slightly and gave the boys a chance to rest. They didn't want to cut the top of the mast completely free until they could see clearly and had a rest. Out of pure exhaustion, they each took one hour of rest. They wanted to be sure not to let the wrong things go when they made their final cuts with the big heavy wire cutters. And Skip remembered Mr. Grey's words, "Measure twice, cut once."

The sun had just peeked over the eastern horizon when the rain stopped for the first time in days. And even though the sun had just come up, the boys could already feel its warmth on their bodies. It was a welcome relief and they took advantage of the slightly calmer weather to go over their plan. They salvaged some of the important pieces of the rigging, some wires, and the masthead lights figuring they might be able to rewire these on their new homemade mast. Then at last, they cut away the top half of the broken mast. It took all of their strength to get it off the boat, and they watched sadly as the heavy aluminum soon sunk to the bottom of the Coral Sea.

Actually, the boys were feeling lucky because the lower part of the mast was still standing. After surveying the situation in the light, Kanek said, "What a mess! Can we make it work?" Skip nodded and began climbing the small fold down steps on the sides of the mast. He had with him tools and a **block and tackle**, which they would rig to hoist the sails. He climbed up and down four times in order to finally get everything set right but by the afternoon, the boys had a small mainsail and a small jib flying. Their hard work had paid off. With a big shout of joy, "Woo-hoo! We have sails again!" they rounded up and steered a course for Australia.

They felt pretty proud of themselves and it seemed as though the rest of the world was smiling at them. The seas had eased down to a mere 5 feet, the winds were down to 15 knots, the sun had broken through, and their cold, weary, and wet bones were finally starting to dry out. It seemed as though once they decided what to do, and had begun taking action, their plan had fallen into place. The process of re-rigging the boat had been difficult but it went fairly smoothly. Finally something was going their way on this passage! Even though they didn't have a full mast, after surviving the storm and re-rigging the boat, they felt they could handle anything else Mother Nature threw at them!

Below in the main cabin, it looked like a bomb had gone off. The rough seas had wreaked havoc on everything stowed away, even in supposedly locked cabinets. There were cans of food, squashed papayas, spilled flour, beans, salt-soaked papers, books, and clothes and everything else the boys owned scattered around the cabin. While picking up items and putting them back in their place, something different caught Kanek's eye. As he bent over to look closer, Kanek saw it was about the size of a baseball, jagged edged, all black, and filled with small air holes. He held it up for Skip to see. "Is this yours?"

"Yeah, I got it at the volcano on Vanuatu. It's a piece of lava from the trail!"

"No! Skip! You didn't bring a piece of the volcano onboard?! Don't you know that makes the spirits angry and brings bad luck?"

"I didn't know," Skip said bowing his head. "I really didn't know. I thought we'd want it as a souvenir," he bumbled out.

"Its okay Skip. I can't be mad at you if you didn't know. But you know other superstitions like not leaving for a passage on a Friday, or not bringing bananas aboard, right? How could you have missed this one?" What do you say we give it back right now?" Together they went up on deck, Skip apologized to the spirits of the volcano, and threw it as far as he could into the depths. "That oughta do it," Kanek said and they both nodded and started to laugh. Perhaps it was because they had been through so much and were giddy from being over-tired and over-worked, but they rolled onto the cockpit floor laughing so hard they were holding their bellies. "As if the spirit of the volcano thinks it's going to beat us!" Kanek shouted. "Not a chance!"

"Mango!" Skip cried! "Where is Mango?" They raced back down below and found Mango in the same closet. She had been knocked off her perch and was flitting about on the floor, walking around in circles seemingly lost.

"Mango oowweee Mango owwweeeee. Mango owwee" Her left wing was crooked. Upon closer inspection, Kanek declared Mango's wing was broken. Kanek could see the was dehydrated and hungry too. They wrapped her in a blanket, gave her water and food and waited for her to go to sleep. Then they used some sticks of wood and wire to make a splint for her wing and wrapped it up as best they could until they could get more professional help.

The boys were also in a bit of shock and numbly did their tasks of keeping the boat sailing on course as best they could. Two days later, while staring into the afternoon sun, Kanek spun around and shouted at the top of his lungs, except only a whisper emerged from his mouth. He waved his hands and pointed, but still only a barely audible whisper came out, "Land! Land Ho! Skip! Land!" The boys jumped up and down with joy! As the sun was dropping low in the west, JULIA pulled up to the city dock at the small town of Boolaba on the low-lying coast of Australia. They were greeted by the harbor master and as they told their story, more and more people swarmed around to see what all the fuss was about. Word spread fast, and soon what seemed like the entire town of Boolaba was singing a traditional Australian song and welcoming the boys down under. "Waltzing Matilda, Waltzing Matilda, you'll come a waltzing Matilda with me…." the townspeople sang, "and he sang as he watched…" And the boys were treated as heroes for they had survived one of the worst storms to hit the Coral Sea in many years.

"How'd you do it? How did you handle that big boat after losing your mast?" asked a reporter from a local newspaper. Skip smiled, looked at Kanek, and answered the reporter, "**I** didn't do it. **WE** did it together."

"But what a disastrous passage," said the reporter. "You lost your spinnaker, your mast, and you could have sunk!"

"I guess that's it," said Skip. "We didn't sink."

With that, Skip and Kanek joined in the singing, "Waltzing Matilda, Waltzing Matilda…"

CHAPTER 11— CROCODILES, SNAKES, AND JELLYFISH...EWW!

S hopping in the great big grocery stores was something Skip was familiar with, but hadn't seen in a long time. Kanek on the other hand, thought he was in a dreamworld. There was an overwhelming selection of fresh, healthy vegetables and fruits compared to what they were able to find in the remote Pacific Islands. In the islands, the boys had been excited at the thought of finding fresh bread in the store. Here, the baker asked, "What kind of bread would you like Mate? Do you want rye, wheat, white, soy, buttermilk, potato, cake, cupcakes, scones, croissants, biscuits...?" Kanek couldn't help but try a bit of them all!

As for getting the boat repaired, they were fortunate to be in a country where boating was taken seriously. The Australians helped the boys tirelessly to install a new mast and rigging, new autopilot, and to fix all of the other broken equipment. In the meantime, the boys enjoyed surfing, swimming, and meeting new friends. But always on their mind was finding Hina. Why did he keep moving? And why did he leave clues? Was he really Boy of the Moon? Or was he a thief? Where was he now and did he really go to Kodo? They saw it written on the cave wall, but why would anybody go to such a dangerous placed as Kodo? Skip and Kanek were eager to find out, and as soon as they were fairly confident cyclone season was over, they headed up the 1500 mile west coast of Australia, bound for Indonesia.

The sailing conditions up Australia's east coast were perfect: warm fresh breezes blew JULIA north at a steady pace across turquoise blue water for as far as the eye could see. The seas were calm because they were sailing inside the Great Barrier Reef rather than out in the open ocean. It was tiring too. Because there were so many reefs, it was too dangerous to sail at night. So by the end of every day, the boys had to find a new anchorage behind a small island or reef. They studied the charts closely to find a safe anchorage from hundreds of choices. They had to consider the wind direction, how the boat would swing on its anchor if the wind direction changed, how close they were to dangerous reefs, and if the sea bottom was good holding ground for the anchor (sand and mud were good, but coral, rocks, gravel, and grass were not). It was hard work but Skip remembered this was an area his hero Captain James Cook spent a lot of time. He found passages through the reefs without charts and without an engine, so Skip figured if Cook could do that, then he could certainly pilot JULIA up the inside channel with charts and GPS for navigation. Besides, this was the fastest way north and now that the weather had shifted in their favor, it was time to get a move-on towards Indonesia and the island of Kodo to find Hina!

One day they crossed a shallow sand bar and had only two feet of water under the keel to spare. Once past the entrance they motored slowly up the Lucky River to anchor in the perfectly calm but dark and muddy river waters. "I read there are lots of crocodiles around here," said Skip, so "please keep all hands and legs inside the vehicle!" They both laughed until they heard a splash. Looking at the muddy riverbank, they saw the last bit of a crocodile tail slither into the water. Another splash nearby and they saw another crocodile enter the water—they weren't laughing anymore. "Can crocodiles climb up the side of the boat?" asked Kanek with his brown eyes wider than Skip had ever seen.

"No, of course not," Skip replied not really sure if he was right. "But I've heard stories of them jumping high out of the water and grabbing people off the sides of their boat as they leaned over. So, no reaching over the side! And Mango, you hear that, stay inside!"

"Stay inside, stay inside, stay inside," Came the response. Mango's wing had healed and she was flying all around the cabin. She even occasionally took off and flew a couple circles around the boat before coming back to her perch, but she seemed to understand this wasn't the place to explore on her own.

As night fell and darkness enveloped the river basin, the sounds and sights became creepier and scarier. They heard what sounded like a slithering sound, then splashes, then gurgling sounds, breathing sounds, thrashing, and squealing. They had no idea what was going on. Was a crocodile attacking a pig? Because that's what it sounded like! Were there snakes? The boys closed all the portholes and hatches before going to bed that night and slept uneasy as they thought of what might be going on in the jungle nearby. The next morning they were up early and both had the same thing in mind. "Let's get out of here!" Kanek said and before the sun had even come up, JULIA was motoring toward the river entrance and back out to sea. What a change in their thinking as they now sought safety at sea!

By noon, they had already covered the 40 miles to Lizard Island, now an inaccurate name because the lizards, which were supposedly two to three feet long, had over thousands of years grown wings and had flown to another island in the south. Rumors said there were so many lizards there, no man would go near the place. But at Lizard Island, all seemed calm and they hoped they could trust the local lore that said saltwater crocs usually don't venture much past about 20 miles offshore. The boys were about 25 miles offshore and they wanted to go swimming in the clear turquoise ocean water and go snorkeling on the nearby reef. Standing on the side of the boat studying the water's surface and looking closely at its inhabitants, both boys were just about ready to jump in when all of a sudden, Skip grabbed Kanek's arm, yanked him backward and shouted, "Wait! What was that?" pointing to a small black spot on the water's surface. The sun's angle had changed just enough so they could see there was another one. Then another one. These black spots were now everywhere, bobbing to the surface and then sinking back below. "Oh noooooo," said Skip taking off his snorkeling gear. "No swimming here. Do you know what those are?" They both looked more closely and now they could make out what the black spots were: the heads of poisonous sea snakes! "I hate snakes," Skip said, and I read that those silver and black striped ones are the most poisonous in the world. One bite and you're toast. Good thing we looked before we leaped!"

No swimming allowed—Crocodiles, Snakes, and Jellyfish, Ewww!

"You hate snakes?" teased Kanek "You sailed all this way, you're the bravest kid I've ever known, and you hate snakes?" He laughed hard but when he saw Skip's head droop down at the teasing, he stopped.

"So I'm afraid of snakes, so what?" said Skip. "Hey, Indiana Jones hates snakes too, and he's braver than both of us put together!"

"You're right, sorry Skip, I just didn't think you were afraid of anything," Kanek said apologetically. "You afraid of anything else I should know about?"

"No, I think that's about it," said Skip quickly turning away. For deep down he knew that his biggest fear was being teased and made fun of. He hated it but he accepted Kanek's apology and they went about making their supper for the evening.

The next afternoon's anchorage was the most beautiful they had seen in Australia. The water was crystal clear and the nearby reef beckoned them to finally do some good snorkeling and fish-watching. Kanek joked, "Wait, let's be sure there's no snakes!"

Skip gave him a dirty look. "Ha-ha, very funny," Skip said as he had already looked for the small black headed creatures bobbing to the surface for air. But now, with the doubt put in his head by Kanek, he leaned over the side and looked closely at the water. The surface was as smooth as glass and reflected the afternoon sky like mirrored windows on the sides of office buildings. But the water was strangely shiny—too glossy—too smooth. Suspicious, Skip grabbed the fishing net, reached over the side and took a big scoop from the water's surface and brought it up to the boat. As he put the net down on the deck, they both stared in amazement at what must have been at least 100 tiny jellyfish just from the one scoop. They looked up their catch in the fish-identifier book and discovered they were surrounded by Irukandji jellyfish, one of the world's most poisonous of all. Another day of no swimming!

Later that afternoon, Skip went below and found Kanek deeply engrossed in the same book. "Says here that Australia has every known poisonous fish, animal, or reptile on the planet. You name your poison and Australia's got it! I don't think we're going to do anymore swimming for a while."

"I love Australia," said Skip, "but without swimming..." he hesitated and then with a laugh, shouted—"Let's get out of here!" "Next stop, Indonesia! Let's Go find Hina!"

"Hey Skip, this book says that Indonesia has tons of poisonous animals, fish, and reptiles…almost as many as Australia!" Skip just rolled his eyes.

"Don't forget we're going to Kodo, said Skip. We're sure to find Brian, I, er, mean Hina there. What's it say about the Kodo dragons Kanek? You know I've always wanted to see the dragons and now we have a great reason to go there!" He had been telling Kanek about the famous Kodo dragons that live in Indonesia. "Well, it says here they grow to more than 15 feet long, and 4 feet around, and they can run up to 15 miles an hour! It also says there are rumors they have wings and can fly!" Kanek's eyes were as wide as saucers as he described how the dragons eat cows and water buffalo. All they have to do is get one bite into their prey and the poison begins to work on shutting down the victim's nervous system. Then the dragons move in and eat the animal as it's dying. "Ewwwwwwwww!" they both shouted at the same time. "I don't know Skip, these sound like they're really dangerous."

"Yeah, why do you suppose Hina went there? I wonder what HE's looking for? "I hope he's still alive and not eaten for lunch by the dragons!"

"Here's the good news Skip. The one thing dragons can't do is swim. They can run and fly, but they can't swim. Let's remember that!

CHAPTER 12—
ISLAND OF THE
DRAGONS

They were lost. Skip and his now official first mate Kanek had been sailing for days in Indonesian waters searching for the mystery island of Kodo, known to be home of the giant Kodo Dragons. Skip had always been fascinated by stories of the mysterious giant reptiles but could never find anybody who had seen them. The books said they existed but nobody had seen one in more than 20 years so perhaps they became extinct? Did they even exist? There were several stories of people who had gone searching for them and didn't return. He was determined to find the dragons and prove they were real. He wanted to be the first one to take photos and document them, especially if they flew. He would be famous! If they didn't eat him first. But his interest in the Kodo dragons wasn't his number one reason for trying to find the island. Hina was supposedly here, or had been here. He had written the word Kodo on the cave wall back in Vanuatu so this must have been his next stop. But when? While the boys went to Australia to make repairs and enjoy the life of beach bums for a few months, Hina could have come and long gone. Who are they going to ask, the first Kodo dragon they run into? "Excuse me, Mr. Dragon, I'm looking for my lost brother named Hina. You'd know him by an upside crescent moon birthmark on his right leg…you know, the one you probably just ate for lunch!"

First things first though; they didn't know where they were. Indonesia is made up of over 1,000 islands and Skip wasn't exactly sure of their position. It wasn't a problem with the GPS—it was working fine. The charts on the other hand, were miles off in their accuracy so they didn't match the actual shapes of the bays and inlets. And to top it off, coral reefs were everywhere blocking their entrance to any safe anchorage.

Even though Skip was lost, he wasn't afraid. He told Kanek the story about when he was younger and had sailed his little boat to the island of Catalania. It was much farther than Avalonia and he had become lost in the fog. All he had to navigate with was his compass, so he held his compass course until the island finally loomed up out of the heavy mist in front of him. He learned to trust his compass and from that moment on, he knew he could be lost and not afraid.

Kanek climbed to the top of their shiny new Australian-made mast and looked west towards a tiny bay they were considering entering. He always liked climbing the mast because it reminded him of his days climbing coconut trees. He was a natural climber and scooted up the mast as if indeed it was a coconut tree.

Skip had a hunch they had found Kodo but he was impatient and instead of sailing around the island looking for a proper anchorage, he wanted to get in through the dangerous reefs to save time. He figured Hina must be gone by now but he had to see if he had been here and left a clue to his next destination. "See any way in?" Skip hollered up to Kanek who was now hanging on with arms and legs wrapped securely around the mast 60 feet above the deck. At that height even the smallest motion of the boat was making the mast sway back and forth more than a coconut tree in a hurricane. But Kanek was a real trooper and in spite of his arms turning numb from gripping so tightly, he knew how important his job was—they had to find a way into a safe anchorage!

"I think I see a narrow break in the reef over there!" Kanek shouted back down to Skip who stood firmly with a tight grip on the huge steering wheel. Kanek had learned from his grandfather how to determine the water's depth by the color of the water, which was reflecting the sea bottom. Real light turquoise, almost white was shallow water over sand, too shallow for JULIA's keel to make it over without running aground. The darker the water, generally the deeper it was except for when the dark water wasn't water at all, but rather huge coral heads. He was hearing his grandfather's teachings as he shouted instructions back down to Skip. "Turn to starboard 45 degrees. That's it, now port 10 degrees, now straight on…" Kanek kept on with his instructions as Skip nimbly steered JULIA between the dangerous reefs that were just waiting to attack the hull and tear her to pieces with razor sharp rocks and coral. The currents were strong and Skip struggled to hold the wheel steady, while high above the deck Kanek gripped the mast in a bear hug holding on for dear life as the currents tossed the boat around like a toy. On they sailed through the narrow pass hoping for clear water ahead. Primitive looking birds with long beaks, sharp teeth, and huge wingspans soared in circles overhead screeching loudly, while some courageously dipped near the boat to investigate this intruder. And then there were the sharks with their big black fins darting back and forth on the surface of the clear shallow water. It wasn't a very friendly welcoming committee. The prehistoric looking birds and unnerving water creatures were giving a warning: "Stay out of this place…danger lurks here!"

Island of the Dragons—Everything about it said 'Danger!'

"Look out Skipper! **Bommie** dead ahead!" shouted Kanek. The turquoise blue lagoon was filled with the huge dark coral heads scattered at random, each one possessing the ability to sink any boat unlucky enough to make contact with it. Skip swung the wheel hard to port and held his breath while Julia heeled over sharply exposing her keel and by the tiniest margin, she barely slipped by the enormous, angry-looking coral head that was the final obstacle to entering the bay. Kanek climbed down from the mast panting, gave Skip a *"Whew, that was close,"* look, and headed forward to where the anchor was stored at the bow of the boat.

"Looks clear and sandy here, let's get the anchor down," Skip called to Kanek. The chain rattled and shook as it ran out of the locker, pulled by the heavy steel anchor…down, down, down it went into the clear water until it struck bottom and dug into the soft sand. For the first time in days Skip and Kanek let out a sigh of relief as they looked around and began absorbing their new surroundings.

The boys were both covered in sweat from their nervous entry into the bay. And it was hot, really hot with typical thick moisture-filled air making it impossible to cool off. Especially since once again, there was no swimming unless they wanted to be shark bait! Huge threatening rainclouds created gloomy shadows that covered the small lagoon with an eerie darkness. The sharks had followed them into the anchorage and were circling with their ever-present threat. The screeching birds overhead added to the wild noises coming from the wild jungle ashore making the boys jump at every new strange sound. The island showed all the signs of a wild, daunting, primeval land: aside from a couple of small sandy beaches, it was all black lava rock from volcanic eruptions but most was now covered in green…all shades of green: bright green, yellow-green, blue-green. "This place gives me the creeps," said Kanek as his small frame shivered in spite of the heat.

"Creeps, Creeps, Creeps shouted Mango as she bobbed frantically up and down. Creeps! Creeps!" She then made her way into the back of the clothes closet where she hid.

"Maybe we should take a hint from Mango, birds and animals have a good sense of danger. I don't think we should be here," said Kanek.

They waited a full day until they had built up enough nerve to venture ashore in the dinghy. Once on the beach, the explorers moved quietly, suspicious of everything they saw and heard. After following a narrow trail into the brush, the trail shifted to the side of a black cliff, which they followed until it flattened out to more jungle. Suddenly, they both paused at the same time. "Did you hear that?" asked Kanek.

"Yeah, it was just one of those birds though," said Skip. "C'mon, let's keep going." Before too long they came to a small clearing with one single coconut tree growing out of the lava rock. As they approached the tree, they both could clearly see the carving. There was Hina's mark, an upside down crescent moon. And right below was carved, "Kodo Yao."

"What do you suppose it means?" asked Kanek.

"I don't know but that's definitely Hina's mark. He was here Kanek!"

They didn't have time to ponder it further because Kanek was already looking at something else. He was knelt over the ground and shaking his head. "Uh, Skipper, you want to have a look over here?" whispered Kanek with a doubting voice. Kanek pointed to the gigantic tracks in the sand. They didn't look like anything they had ever seen before. Each print was a foot across with toes that looked more like claws. The prints alternated left, right, left, right, with a line in the sand down the middle…the line of a tail being dragged? Kanek looked up at Skip, his big brown eyes again wide as saucers with a questioning look. "Let's get out of here Skip. I don't like this place."

"It's them. I just know it. We found the dragons," Skip said with a strange wild gleam in his eye. It was a look Kanek hadn't seen before and he got goose bumps on his arms. "C'mon, let's follow the tracks," Skip said as he knelt down and silently tiptoed forward. Kanek crouched behind him as they gently moved ahead into the thick jungle. "Shhh," said Skip, "I think I hear something up ahead."

As the boys crept forward into the brush, the noises grew louder. "Let's go," Kanek pleaded. "Let's just turn around and go. This is crazy." But Skip couldn't turn back now, not after all it took to get this far. He might have found the Kodo Dragons! They didn't have to wait long. As Skip pulled apart the branches of a bush, there right in front of them, not more than 50 yards away, was a scene straight out of the movies. Three giant Kodo Dragons lay on the ground gnawing away at their lunch, which looked like the remains of an enormous water buffalo. Skip had read that water buffalo weigh about 2,000 pounds—that's a ton—it must have taken some aggressive hunters to take it down! The scene was really gross: the buffalo's horns still poked up out of its half-eaten head and body, and the dragons munched away as if they were having an enjoyable afternoon picnic. Each one was about 15 feet long and 4 feet around. They looked like giant iguanas and they snapped at each other over the various pieces of buffalo, like children arguing over the last cookie at dessert. When they moved around their picnic site in order to munch on a different part of the body, their yellow forked tongues darted in and out of their huge drooling mouths that hung half open exposing their big yellow alligator like teeth. Skip had heard rumors that their saliva was poisonous so once they had a taste of their prey it was all over for the hunted. They used their enormous sharp clawed feet to injure their target, and followed their victims, sometimes for days until the wounded animal, humans included, collapsed from the poison. It was a gruesome site but the boys couldn't pry their eyes away and stared for a couple of minutes. Skip whispered to Kanek explaining this was the food chain in action and only the strongest survived. "Yeah, that's great," Kanek whispered back, "But can we not be part of that food chain please?"

Click, click, click was the sound of Skip's camera as he shot dozens of pictures of the dragons. While the dragons hadn't heard the boys whispers, they did here the sound of the camera. One of them looked up from its meal, cocked its head to the left, slowly raised itself to its claw-feet, and started lumbering towards the boys' hiding place. Now it was Skip's turn to say, "Let's get outta here. Run!" and the two of them took off running back the way they came through the jungle. They heard rustling behind them, lots of rustling. When they looked back, they saw not one, but two Kodo Dragons chasing them. While the dragons looked like they would be slow, they weren't. Like crocodiles, they were running fast, way faster than two boys with sea legs could and the dragons were gaining on them! "Faster, faster!" shouted Skip until finally the boys made it to the trail, they slowed down thinking the dragons would back off, but they didn't. They kept coming! The dragons were looking at them as dessert to their water buffalo meal! They had made it back to the cliffside trail, which was only about 2 feet wide along the steep cliff.

On one side was a drop-off of about 100 feet into a ravine. On the other was the steep cliff almost straight up.

They looked over their shoulders and saw the dragons gaining on them. What was it going to be, down the ravine or cliff climbing? They were out of options as the dragons were closing in on them too fast. They had to make a decision NOW! They stopped running and turned to face the steep rock wall. "C'mon, Let's Go! Up, up, up!" shouted Skip. Grabbing at anything and everything: rock outcrops, clumps of grass, a bush here, a branch there, they scrambled up 20 feet above the trail. There they stopped and looked at each other. "Hold on Kanek, you can do it, hold on," Skip said.

"Me?! Don't you remember I climb coconut trees!" said Kanek nervously. Only moments later, the dragons arrived below, stopped, looked up, and stared as if to say, "We'll come back for you later!" For the longest minute in history, the boys clung to the rock wall while the dragons paced back and forth beneath them as if they were waiting for the boys to lose their grip and fall into their mouths. Finally, the dragons decided the boys weren't worth the effort, turned, and lumbered slowly back to their original meal. Had they been hungrier, they would have put in more effort, but they still had a water buffalo to finish. After the dragons had been long gone for at least two minutes, the boys slid down the rock face, scraping and cutting their skin and not even caring. Their feet hit the trail and they took off running toward the beach where they had left the dinghy. They leaped into the boat, started the outboard motor and zoomed out to where JULIA sat anchored. Aaahhh, JULIA, the safe house, their sanctuary, the place where no dragons could ever reach.

As they flopped onto the boat, Kanek turned to Skip and calmly said, "NOW are you convinced there are dragons?!"

"Yeah, I am," said Skip, "and I'm glad the rumors of them flying aren't true. We have to go back, I want to get some better pictures." That started an argument that went on for a couple of hours with Skip pleading his case to go back and photograph the dragons versus Kanek's desire to pull up the anchor and sail away from Kodo. "Come on Kanek, don't you trust me?" That was the wrong question to ask because Kanek just turned and looked the other way.

It was mid-afternoon when their decision was made for them. Skip was fiddling with his camera, getting it ready for their next trip ashore when they heard a loud "Screech!" sound. Over and over they heard it but couldn't tell where it was coming from. They kept staring at the island looking for movement when out of nowhere, they saw a huge shadow sweep across the water in front of them. A shadow on the water? That could only mean something was above them.

"Look up there!" shouted Kanek pointing to the sky. There were the three Kodu dragons, their hidden wings now exposed, flying in circles around the boat screeching violently signifying they were about to attack. The boys crawled slowly to safety under the sun canopy so the dragons couldn't see them.

"So it's true, they *can* fly!" Skip started snapping pictures like crazy. When one swooped down low to the water, Skip got some great shots as the dragon turned its head and looked at him eye to eye as it flew by. "Okay, I got my pics," said Skip. "We could go now but how are we going to go on deck to pull up the anchor. Those things could swoop down and pick us up like a fish!"

"We're trapped," said Kanek thinking out loud. "Maybe we can wait 'em out, or leave at night."

"We can't go through that reef at night," said Skip. *"Think Skip, think!"* he was pounding the palm of his hand against his forehead as if that was going to knock the idea out of his head. They decided to wait rather than risk going up on deck. Unfortunately, the dragons seemed patient and when they weren't circling overhead, they landed on the beach and sat there watching with a dutiful eye to see if the boys were going to make a mistake. Soon, darkness came over the lagoon like a dark veil. There was no moon so there was no chance of making it out through the reef at night. Besides, the boys could see the red eyes of the dragons sitting on the beach. Maybe they were discussing what else they should have with their meal of two boys!

It was a long and restless night and the boys stood watch as if they were at sea just to be sure that no creature was sneaking onto the boat while they slept below. While they were trying to figure out how they were going to escape from the dragons, Skip buried his head in some of the sailing guidebooks. He was looking for the words, Kodo Yao and it didn't take long to find out what they meant. "Hey, guess what Kanek? Remember the carving on the tree? Kodo Yao is an island! And it's in Thailand! That must be where Hina went."

"If he didn't get eaten by the dragons," said Kanek.

"He didn't, I can feel it," whispered Skip. "I just know he's still alive and look, here's Kodo Yao on the chart. That's where he is and that's where we're going next!" They confirmed the location with the fist-sized template and sure enough, Kodo Yao in Thailand was exactly correct.

"How could I be so stupid?" ranted Skip. The clue said Kodo and you even asked about the 'Y' and the scratches in the rock. I just ignored that part of the clue because I was too excited about Kodo. What a dummy I am! And now we're going to be lunch for the dragons!" Skip didn't sleep much and they were up at first light. Skip put the binoculars up to his eyes and stared at the beach. Sure enough, there were the three dragons still on the beach licking their chops at the thought of having the two boys for breakfast. As he watched, one of the dragons ran down the beach, spread its wings and took off into the air, flew out over the boat and took up position circling overhead. Around and around it flew, waiting patiently. There seemed to be no way out for Skip and Kanek. They were trapped on the boat and in the lagoon. They couldn't fight the dragons, and they didn't know how to chase them away, so they waited. They waited and waited until the day had passed and turned to night again. They stood watch again and were starting to get really scared as they thought they might just be stuck in that lagoon until they became dragon food.

The next morning, as the sun came up over the horizon, Skip saw something very strange coming towards them in the water. There was lots of splashing and what appeared to be huge creatures swimming through the water. Then Skip saw huge fins sticking up out of the water at least 3 feet into the air. "Sharks!" he shouted down below. Kanek came running up to the cockpit and looked to where Skip was pointing. He grabbed the binoculars from Skip, brought them up to his eyes and stared out to sea at the commotion in the water. He not only saw big black creatures swimming toward them, but he thought he also saw big fish jumping out of the water. As the whole parade of huge beasts swam toward them and into the lagoon, Kanek shouted, "Orca! Those aren't sharks, they're Orca—you know, killer whales—and they're friendly! And those huge fish aren't fish, they're bottlenose dolphins—hundreds of them!

"Killer whales?" asked Skip with a raised eyebrow?

"Actually they're all dolphins, including the Orca. They're all part of the same dolphin family. My grandfather used to tell me stories of the great mariners before us, who sailed from my homeland Tahiti to New Zealand. When they were in trouble or lost at sea, it was the dolphins that saved them every time." As they spoke, four of the giant Orca, each one nearly as long as the boat, began swimming slowly in a circle around JULIA, forming a protective ring no creature could get past from the water. At one point, they stopped the circles and began breeching out of the water showing their huge mouths and teeth as they leapt high in the air. There was no fish, animal, or reptile on the planet that could mess with the Orca, and they were clearly showing off to the dragons as if to say, "Don't even try it." As they were breeching, the bottlenose dolphins formed another ring inside the whales traveling twice their speed, leaping in and out of the water breathing loudly through their blowholes on the top of their heads. The enormous amount of splashing churned up the rich minerals and salt in the water creating a layer of foam on the water's surface, as if hands were splashing in a bubble bath. While they were under water, the dolphins began "bubble hunting," blowing large bubbles of oxygen out their blowholes. As a group, they use these bubbles to heard their prey into the mouths of fellow dolphins. They usually only blow enough oxygen for the bubbles to last until they reach the surface and then they pop. But today was different and the whole school of dolphins worked together blowing bigger bubbles that picked up the foam from the surface. The bubbles accelerated upwards so fast that when they broke the surface, they launched at high speed into the air with such force they could knock an airplane out of the sky. It was a sight to behold and the boys stared in amazement at the giant ring of foamy bubbles extending so high into the sky, they couldn't see where it ended. The orca and dolphins' bubble ring formed a protective barrier that couldn't be penetrated from the sea or the air and JULIA was now secure in her own fortress. The boys just stared in amazement at the scene unfolded in front of them.

The Kodo dragons had been watching but they appeared ready for battle, as soon all three had taken up positions circling in the sky above. The dragons had never seen anything like the bubble ring and had no idea what they were up against. The first dragon tucked its wings, dropped its head and went into a high-speed dive headed straight for Kanek on the bow of the boat. Skip shouted, "Kanek, look out! Get down!" Kanek threw himself flat on the deck grabbing onto the rail like super glue. He turned his head to the sky and saw the dragon headed right for him. He held on tight but prepared for the worst. The dragon's yellow eyes were wide and its ears streamed back as it dove towards the boat. Just a few seconds more and its claws would be snatching Kanek from the deck. As the dragon screeched toward JULIA, the dolphins' activity took on a frenzy of its own. The dolphins were now blowing thousands of giant bubbles at such high speed it was as if they were a wall of cannon balls being shot into the air. The dragon dove faster and faster toward the boys and Kanek thought for sure he was a goner. Neither the boys or the dragon knew the high mineral and salt content made the bubbles virtually unbreakable. All of a sudden they heard a crash like a car slamming into a cement wall. They looked up and saw the dragon crumble as it was stopped cold by the wall of bubbles. Still screeching, it tumbled and rolled down and made a loud splash as it fell limp into the water. Its last squeals came just before the Orca tore it to bits. The dragon's blood in the water attracted at least a dozen grey sharks and they went into a feeding frenzy. They knew better than to mess with the dolphins and Orca and were content having dragon for lunch.

Skip and Kanek were still trying to figure out what was going on when a fifth orca bumped the side of the boat gently with its nose. Then it swam slowly forward to the bow, paused, and broached 20 feet out of the water. It did this again and again, then swam further forward and broached again. The boys stared in wonder until Kanek got it. "Skip! Skip! They're here to save us. Look, the Orca wants us to follow it!" Skip's mouth dropped open in amazement until all he could utter was, "Let's go!" They brought up the anchor as fast as they could, Skip slipped the boat into forward gear, and they motored slowly toward the pass in the reef. While the dolphins and Orca kept up their protective circle, the biggest Orca led the way through the reef and out of the lagoon. The two remaining dragons circled high in the air screeching in protest but there was nothing they could do to stop the boys from leaving. They couldn't penetrate the bubbles by air nor could they swim past the Orca.

As the sails went up and caught the wind, JULIA headed to sea, and the dragons retreated back toward the island.

The dolphins stayed with the boys for about an hour and they seemed to know when it was safe to leave. The biggest bottlenose and the biggest Orca both remained with them swimming alongside. There was something very compelling about these animals and the boys even started talking to them. As if hypnotized, the boys stared into their eyes thanking them, and found themselves drawn to them with a very close bond. Kanek was talking to the giant Orca, thanking it for helping when he noticed something familiar. He was looking at the Orca's right side and it's eye kept twitching and then it would blink very fast, especially when Kanek was quiet, as if the whale was saying something through its eye. On the other side of the boat, Skip was engrossed in his own one-way conversation with the big bottlenose dolphin. Both were so absorbed with the animals, it seemed as if they were talking to old friends. As the rescuers swam alongside, Skip suddenly let go of the wheel, his arms went limp, his jaw dropped, and he just stared at the dolphin. He was looking closely at three white streaks on its left cheek. It looked like a giant cat had scratched the dolphin and left a scar. But before Skip could get another word out of his mouth, both animals made giant leaps into the air as if saying farewell, and then in a flash they were gone. The boys looked at each other in silence. They tried to speak but no words formed. Then at the same they blurted out the same question, "Who were you talking to?!"

Kanek answered first. "It was the strangest thing. As I was looking into the giant eye on the orca, I all of a sudden saw someone. The eyes looked so familiar, but nah, it couldn't be."

"What? Who was it?" Skip asked demandingly. "Who? I have to know. I have to know if what just happened really happened?"

"Well, I know it sounds weird," said Kanek as he looked down, "But do you remember me telling you about my grandfather's twitch in his eye? That whale had the same twitch and I could have sworn I was talking with my grandfather."

Skip shook his head and said, "No, it couldn't be, it just couldn't be." He looked around for the Orca and bottlenose but they were both gone.

"Why Skip? What are you talking about?" "What is it Skip? Who was it? WHO were you talking to?"

"I don't know how to explain it," Skip whispered. His eyes were wide "It couldn't be, could it? Do you remember when I told you about the scar on my mom's cheek?"

CHAPTER 13—THE CLOSEST CALL OF ALL

Indonesia, Singapore, Malaysia, and then Thailand…even the names sounded exotic to Skip. And while Kanek was from an island country, Tahiti was tiny compared to the vastness of southeast Asia. At first, these faraway lands felt strange. The food was different, the languages sounded nothing like they had heard before, and the pace of living was slow, peaceful, and calm compared to the fast pace of the big cities of Australia. But they were getting used to change. Moving from anchorage to anchorage, ocean to ocean, and country to country was showing them the world was more than cars, freeways, and hamburgers. Skip and Kanek discovered the people in these countries all had one thing in common—they were happy—almost suspiciously so. They weren't rich, didn't live in fancy houses, most didn't own cars but instead rode their bikes or motor scooters (one day, they saw a family of five people riding down the street on one motor-scooter!). They didn't wear expensive clothes, didn't go to dress-up dinners, and they seemed more focused on how others were doing, than about themselves. The local people the boys met always went out of their way to say hello and offer assistance in their ever-present quest for food, spare parts, repairs, and sightseeing. In one of the shops they met Ning, a shy and ever so nice girl about their age who helped them find what they needed. The shop was owned by her parents and Ning and her brother Pia pretty much ran the store day to day together. They got along well with Ning and all became fast friends.

Every country visited required an official check-in with customs, and Thailand was no exception. They received the usual strange questioning looks from the officials as they explained how they were looking for Skip's lost brother and were on "official business" from Skip's mother for the mission. Skip even showed them the letter from his mom instructing him to "Find Brian and reunite with your brother." As usual, after many questions, the boys were officially entered into the country. As they walked out of the customs office, the officials just shook their heads and shrugged their shoulders. This made the boys stand a bit taller as they were very proud of being such young adventurers.

Their first order of business was to find the island of Kodo Yao. It was shown on the chart, but Skip wanted to see if they could pick up some local knowledge about the island and anchorages. Kanek just wanted to be sure there were no dragons anywhere near the island! Who would know the area best? Fishermen were always the best source of local knowledge for boating as they spent every day out on the water. So the boys headed down to the beach where the longtail fishing boats were pulling in from their days at sea. The boats were so named because they had a car engine sitting at the back of the boat, and a long drive shaft of about 10-15 feet with the propeller on the end. They maneuvered the boats by moving the drive shaft which changed the boat's direction. The boys started to relax as they heard the fisherman give good reports about the island of Kodo Yao. But the fishermen were curious why the boys wanted to go there as it was uninhabited. Why would Hina go to an unpopulated island? While it might be a good place to escape to, with no people or community, what would be the draw for Brian to go there? Kanek rolled his big brown eyes and looked suspiciously at Skip. "If you're taking us to another prehistoric island filled with more scary monsters, you can just count me right out!" But the fishermen assured the boys there were no such monsters so they made plans to set sail the next day.

As it turns out, the island was only a one-day sail away. The waters of Phang Nga Bay were emerald green and the sailing was easy with light winds and calm waters protected by the close proximity of land.

The sailing was uneventful which was just fine with the boys. Anchoring was easy in a beautiful flat water bay surrounded by lush greenery, dramatic limestone cliffs, and even a white sand beach at the head of the bay. They were in paradise!

The next day they ventured ashore where Skip discovered that part of the beach was covered in flat stones perfect for skipping. He and Kanek spent hours perfecting their skills while discussing how to go about looking for Hina on an empty island with no people. "I can understand why Hina would come here, but not sure why he would stay," Skip said. "How would he eat? What would he do all day? Who would he talk to?"

"I have another question," asked Kanek. How did he get here in the first place? Who brought him here? And if he left, how did he get off of the island? Somebody must have dropped him off here and if he left, somebody must have picked him up."

"The fishermen!" Skip blurted out. "We didn't ask them about Hina and I'll bet they know. We have to go back and ask the fishermen."

"Let's at least look for him first. He seems to be pretty good at leaving clues, and we should at least try," Kanek added. "Besides, don't you think we should stay in paradise for a while?" For the first time in a long while, Skip and Kanek truly relaxed. There were no monsters or storms to worry about and for the next two days, the boys played on the beach, explored all over the island, picked fresh fruit, and didn't run into a single scary animal. They even let Mango out and watched her fly and stretch her newly healed wing. She seemed so happy and so did the boys. Skip didn't want to admit it out loud, but he was thinking about how he was enjoying himself, and was starting to ask himself why he was chasing Hina? And the same questions as before ate at him. Why was Hina running, why was he leaving clues, and why didn't he want to be found? Was Hina just messing with them and leading them on a wild goose chase?

While exploring, the boys discovered another carving. The letters K-O-D-O were cut into a coconut palm tree in the most conspicuous place, which clearly showed whoever did the carving wanted it to be seen. At the end of the word was a carved arrow that pointed back to the first letter K, as if to say the word was backwards or something like that. The boys were puzzled. They sat on the beach drawing the word in the sand over and over again until all of a sudden Skip leaped up and shouted, "I've got it! ODOK!

"What the heck is ODOK?" Asked Kanek.

"You mean where is ODOK. ODOK is a place, that's what," Skip said excitedly. "It's in the Middle East, on the Arabian Sea. I remember it from geography class in school. It's a big oil seaport in Oman. I don't think you're going to like this part though. I remember reading in the paper about it. It's home to pirates, and they pretty much rule the seas in that part of the world. But that's gotta be where Hina is, in Odok!" Suddenly he was excited to find his brother again.

Skip sat back down on the beach and looked at Kanek. "The pirates won't bother us, we're just two kids out for a sail. What would they want with us?" Kanek nodded but wasn't so sure he really agreed with Skip's assessment of the situation. Skip promised to show him where Odok was on the chart—all the way across the Indian Ocean, about a 20-day sail away.

They had been in Thailand for over a month now. And while they loved the beautiful cruising waters of the area, had realized they had better haul JULIA out of the water to work on the bottom of the boat. They went back and forth now with their motivation to find Hina. They were starting to forget why they were even looking for him. "Do we have to haul out, Skip?" asked Kanek. They had such a good time at their anchorage at Patong, neither really wanted it to end. Patong Beach was 2 miles of pure white soft sand and the water was a smooth, dreamy turquoise-blue color that beckoned swimming and playing all day long. And there were no snakes, jellyfish, or crocodiles! The locals were super friendly and it was easy to make friends here. They didn't want to leave, but knew if this work didn't get done soon, they'd be doing it somewhere else at a higher cost. This was also where Ning's shop was and they found themselves hanging out with her and her family more and more.

"I know it's hard to leave this bay, but Thailand is a good place to do this work. It's inexpensive, there are knowledgeable people here, and there's a boat yard with all of the equipment we need."

"I guess you're right," Kanek shrugged, but I'll sure miss this beach!" The next day, they motored JULIA up the east side of the island of Phuket, into a bay, then up a river, and finally stopped at a small dock in front of a run-down boatyard. It was filled with boats sitting high off the ground in steel cradles, dozens of workers scraping, painting, drilling, and hammering. The sign in front needed paint but they could make out its name, Ratanachya. "Looks more like "rats-nest" if you ask me, said Kanek.

In spite of how the yard looked, the workers were professional and clearly knew what they were doing. Before the boys knew it, JULIA was sitting in a cradle rolling up a ramp out of the water on a railroad track. At the top of the track, a squeaky old electric winch was moaning and groaning as it strained to haul the heavy load out of the water. Then there was some juggling of boats on the network of train tracks that lay in the yard. It was like one of those puzzler games where you have to move the letters around, except with boats in a shipyard. By late afternoon, the boys were hot, sweaty, and ready to call it a day. Tomorrow the hard work would begin.

For two weeks, the boys worked alongside the boat workers sanding, painting, drilling, shopping for parts, replacing broken wires, cracked hoses, and corroding metal. "I can't believe how much damage salt water does to just about anything it touches," said Kanek. "It seems like everything needs replacing." It was hot and sweaty living on the boat in the yard and when the boys would awaken in the middle of the night, they had to remember not to jump over the side as if they were anchored—it was a long way down to the hard cement of the boatyard! That night, Skip said, "I wonder Ning and her family are on Patong Beach. Probably having a great time, let's take a **Tuk-Tuk** over to see them tomorrow," and with that the boys fell fast asleep. Life seemed pretty good right about then.

"What's that noise?" Kanek asked as he jumped out of his bunk. It was a deep, rolling thunder-like sound that was quickly becoming louder. The boys popped their head out the hatch and in the early morning sun, saw people running away, many shouting, some screaming, some carrying children—but all were running the same direction—towards the hills. Suddenly an incredibly loud siren began wailing. EeeeeUuuuu uuuuAaaaaaaaaaEeeeeeeeeeeHhhh!

"What's that siren? I've never heard that before!" Skip shouted over the noise. After the siren began screeching, they saw throngs of people running for the hills. Then they heard what the others already knew. At first, it was a soft swishing sound, and then the noise grew in intensity until it sounded like the rushing waters of a raging river. Puzzled, they looked at the hordes of people running for the hills, then at the river where they had hauled JULIA out of the water, and Kanek put it all together.

"I've heard that siren back home. It's a tsunami warning!" Kanek shouted at the top of his lungs.

"Quick, run for the hills!" Skip shouted as he started scrambling over the side and down the 20-foot ladder to the ground.

"No Skip, wait! Look!" Skip stared in amazement where Kanek was pointing—at the river. The water had already flooded up and over the bank and was rushing into the boatyard faster than anybody could run. Workers were climbing poles, trees, scaffolding, and scrambling up onto the boats rather than down from them! "What are we going to do," asked Kanek?"

"Not much we can do now except stay aboard." Just then Skip saw 3 workers running toward their boat. One had a bundle in his arms and they were shouting for help. "Hurry Kanek, get some lines over the side so they can grab on!" At that very moment, the water grabbed the base of their ladder, twisted it, and sent it rushing away in the violent currents that were racing through the boatyard. The three workers had grabbed onto the lines and were barely hanging on when Skip saw that the bundle was a scared and shaking little puppy. The two boys worked together getting the lines wrapped around the big winch, then started cranking it with all their might. Slowly, one by one, they brought the workers aboard and they all flopped into the cockpit exhausted. "*Khob-kun Krub*," they all said in unison, (thank you in Thai).

The five of them and the shaking puppy sat stranded in the cockpit. They could hear Mango down below screeching and then saw her climb into the closet to hide. They couldn't get off the boat so all they could do was hope that the steel cradle JULIA was sitting in would hold. If not, the raging waters would surely toss the boat around like a cork smashing it to bits with all of them onboard. They watched in horror as the water level rose and swept people off their feet. They saw nearby buildings get pounded as the water broke windows, knocked down doors, and sent furniture floating. The lighter weight boats in the yard had already been caught up in the flood and were being sent to a violent end as they crashed into the yard buildings, cranes, and cradles. Then Kanek had an idea.

"We're on a boat, right?" shouted Kanek excitedly.

"Yeah, what do you have in mind?"

"Lower the anchor and put out 100 feet of chain."

"But the ground is cement, how will the anchor dig in?"

"There are railroad tracks all over this yard, right? Kanek said with his eyes lighting up. And they crisscross the yard like a tic-tac-toe game…!"

"Do it! We don't have much time." Skip caught Kanek's enthusiasm as Kanek raced to the foredeck. He unlatched the safety, opened up the windlass, and let her rip! Out flew the anchor and the heavy chain followed until Kanek tightened it up and re-locked the safety catch. "All we can do now is wait," Skip said.

Then, as quickly as the water had rushed in, it ran back out faster than a draining toilet bowl. But as the workers scrambled to try and lower themselves down the ropes, Skip said, "No, wait! Look!" This time the raging water wasn't messing around and began flooding back in twice as fast as the first wave. The brown boiling water surrounded the steel cradle that held JULIA, and the water rose higher and higher until the cradle twisted and broke like it was made of toothpicks. With a huge crash and splash, the boat fell down out of the broken cradle into the water. In an instant, JULIA went from grounded in her cradle, to floating in a river of torrential floodwaters. The water tore at her and pulled and pushed and swirled, and the boat was tossed around like a cork in a bathtub. All five were holding on for dear life as JULIA bounced into other boats and even cars floating in the turbulent waters. She was being pushed quickly toward the steel warehouse and would surely break up if she smashed into the rigid building. "Hold on!" shouted Skip.

The closest call of all—Tsunami!

Suddenly, as if someone had slammed on the brakes of a runaway freight train, JULIA came to a grinding halt throwing everybody forward into the cabin top. The water swirled by them headed for the warehouse, but JULIA held firm. Her anchor chain was tighter than a stretched rubber band and as soon as they realized what had happened, they cheered. "Woo-hoo! It worked!" Kanek said. We're anchored to a railroad track!" Sure enough, in the new, brown deep water that covered the boatyard sat JULIA, anchor chain pointed out ahead and riding the waters as if it were a wild storm. But the anchor held, and as the waters slowly calmed, JULIA settled down and swung peacefully around on her chain as if she were anchored back at Patong Bay.

"Way to go Kanek! But this deep water isn't going to last and when it flows out again, we're going to be high and dry and crash to the cement below. Prepare to raise the anchor!" Kanek knew he had no time to spare and ran forward to bring the anchor up. Skip reached down to the engine starter button, said, "Please, oh please start," and pressed the button. Oh what a beautiful sound that was as the engine coughed, and choked, and then roared to life! As soon as Kanek gave Skip the 'Thumbs Up" meaning the anchor had been brought up to the water's surface, Skip swung the wheel hard over, gave the engine full throttle and JULIA took off across the flooded boatyard toward the deep waters of the river. Once they reached the middle of the river, they again anchored JULIA and watched the last of the waters recede from the boatyard.

Uncertain if another wave was coming, all they could do was hope the tsunami was done causing its overwhelming devastation with two waves. They kept the engine running all night in case they had to quickly move to another place, and it provided power for batteries, lights, radio, and the stove. All five people pitched in to make some hot food, feeling very fortunate to have survived the closest brush with death any of them ever had. Even the puppy seemed happy and he wagged his tail at the food put in front of him. He had made friends with Mango, and they played and hopped around with Mango sitting on the puppy's back like two happy kids.

The next day, the boys dropped their guests off, puppy and all, at the now twisted and mutilated dock at the boatyard. After somber goodbyes, the boys motored slowly to a quiet anchorage behind the island of Phi Raj where they tried to absorb what they had just experienced. Thousands and thousands of people lost their lives, many more thousands lost their homes, possessions, businesses, friends, and families. It was a tragedy of such epic proportion, it was hard to believe it actually happened.

A few days later, the boys were walking along Patong Beach where they had made many friends including Ning and her family, other shop owners, restaurant owners, and beach goers. The shoreline looked worse than if a bomb had hit. Everything including Ning's store, restaurants, houses, and apartment buildings, was flattened within a mile of the beach. As they surveyed the damage and spoke with survivors, the boys discovered they too had lost friends. It made them both so sad they sat down on the now discolored brown littered beach and cried. They cried not only from sadness, but also with relief. Because as they gazed out at Patong Bay, it occurred to them they would have been anchored right there if they hadn't hauled JULIA out of the water. And as they looked around, they couldn't help but notice that every boat they saw was up on the beach and wrecked. That would have been their fate.

"Skip! Kanek!" came the high voice. Over here! It was their friend Ning. With her brown skin, big brown eyes, and long black hair, she could have easily been mistaken for Kanek's sister. She had learned to speak English while selling souvenirs to the tourists, and she and the boys had become good friends during their time in Thailand. Ning sat down next to them, put her head down, and through her tears, explained how her mother, father, and little brother Piya had disappeared after the second wave of the great tsunami. "They didn't believe there would be a second wave," sobbed Ning, "so they didn't run when they should have." All three hugged and cried. Through their tears it felt good to let go, to release their emotions and have a good meltdown.

After a few minutes of silence they were startled to hear Ning say, "Take me with you. Please, I have nothing left here and I will be sad forever if I stay here. Please take me with you."

"But your little brother, what about him? They haven't found his body so there's still hope isn't there?" Skip asked.

"Nobody has heard from him. They can't find him. He must have drowned too," weeped Ning

"Gee I don't know," Skip hesitated as he could feel that old distrust of people rise up in him.

"Well I do," Kanek stood up tall and piped in. "Skip, when I had nothing, you took me in and it's been the best thing that ever happened to me. I trusted you and you trusted me. Now Ning is in the same situation. We have to take her. We want to take her. Will you trust me, just this once for a change?" He glared at Skip as if to say, *'Don't you dare say no.'*

"Oh please Skip," I'm a hard worker and I've been on fishing boats around here, so I know my way around a boat. I'll be a good crew, I promise!"

Skip couldn't resist the two sets of brown eyes staring at him. As a smile spread across his face, he simply said, "Welcome aboard the good ship JULIA."

The three of them jumped up and down and hugged and before long, Ning had moved aboard, taken the third and last cabin aboard JULIA, and was already proving that indeed, she was a hard worker and good crew. And most importantly, Skip noticed she was smiling again. "When do we leave Thailand?" Ning asked. She was eager to put the devastation and sadness behind her.

"We'll go in two days if that's enough time for you," Skip said. They had already provisioned the boat with enough food and supplies to get them all the way across the Indian Ocean and had repaired all of the damage caused by the tsunami. They were ready to go but wanted to leave Ning enough time to say goodbye to her cousin who lived in a small village in the hills untouched by the waters of the tsunami.

It took Ning an extra day to find her way back to the boat through the crowds of humanity. It seemed that everyone was looking for friends and relatives, and phone and Internet lines were still down causing the whole situation to be chaotic. On the third day, when she showed up at the boat, Skip and Kanek were relieved she was all right. She had found her cousin Sarawut, said her goodbyes, and was ready to go. "All right then," Captain Skip said, "Let's go!" And with that, JULIA sailed away from Thailand and began the long journey across the Indian Ocean.

CHAPTER 14— CAMELS AND OIL

The Indian Ocean was a challenge for the three crew of JULIA. Day after day of heavy winds, light winds, and ocean currents that were sometimes in their favor but mostly against them had kept them hard at work. Now Skip, Kanek, and Ning were exhausted from what they called the washing machine effect; choppy and confused seas that caused the boat to bounce up and down, back and forth, side to side, front to back, and every which way. There was no pattern to the sloppy seas. It seemed that the waves were coming from all directions and it made life aboard pretty miserable.

"Oh noooo…not another one," moaned Ning, as an egg resting on the counter went flying across the galley and splattered on the floor making a big mess. Skip saw Ning's frustration and grabbed a towel to help wipe up the raw egg before it became sticky.

"Don't worry about the egg Ning, but try to put them in a more secure spot while cooking," Skip said like a patient teacher would. Just then a wave hit the boat hard from the port side, the boat lurched to starboard, throwing them all into the cabinet on the side of the main salon. "Are you all right?" asked Skip.

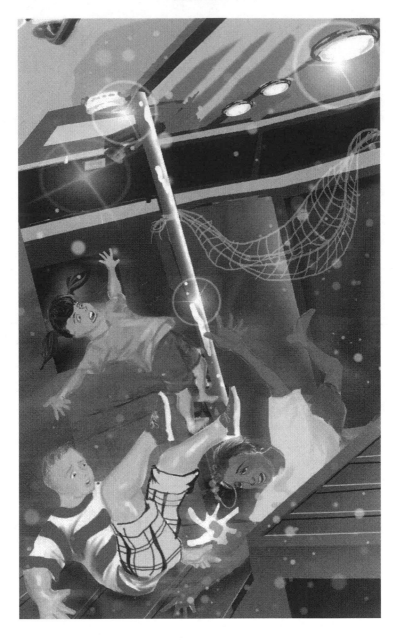

Sailing on the Indian Ocean was like being inside of a washing machine!

"Aaaarrrgggghhhhh!" shouted Ning. Her brown eyes were wide and scary-looking as her yell echoed around the cabin. "This is so frustrating!" Kanek picked himself up off the floor with egg dripping off his arm.

"I know, I know, but be patient," replied Skip. "Remember my spilled spaghetti last night? It's starting to drive me crazy too, but there's not much we can do about it is there? We don't have any choice. We have to keep going. Remember, it's an adventure, and even though it's tough going, we just have to get tougher. If we can't change the situation we're in, then we have to adjust our attitude and how we react to what's happening. The only thing we can really change is our attitude." Skip suddenly stopped talking and said to himself, *"Where did **that** lecture come from? Was that **me** talking?"*

Kanek picked up the conversation. "He's right you know. I used to feel frustrated too. But then I started thinking about what we're doing, where we are, and how amazing it all is. I figured there must be a price for that and I'm willing to suffer through some hard times to be out here. And, just think about how good it will feel when we finally do step ashore in Odok!" They were headed to Odok to look for Hina but it also happened to be the closest port for fuel and the tanks were running low. They had been using the engine because of the extremely light winds and even with the solar panels, they still had to run the generator every day to charge the batteries. The batteries powered nearly everything onboard including the autopilot, radar, instruments that showed boat and wind speed, the radios that were used for communication and to download weather forecasts, pumps, lights, and computers used for navigating and email. It was critical to keep the batteries charged up, and that took fuel to power the generator. So, they had to go where the nearest fuel was—and in this case—it was conveniently Odok.

"I hope you're right about Oman being a safe country," said Kanek. "Are we getting near where the pirates hang out? Isn't that where 'Pirate Alley' is?"

"Well, yeah, I've heard the same thing from other boats on the radio net," said Skip. But I also heard the pirate area doesn't begin until **Oman** and then goes on for about 300 miles to Yemen. So we should be okay for now, let's worry about that later, okay?" Just then the radio crackled to life.

"Little boat, little boat at position North Latitude 14 degrees, East Longitude 64 degrees...please change your course 40 degrees to port." Skip and Kanek looked at each other with a look of, *"He means us!"*

Skip grabbed the microphone and clicked the talk button. "This is the sailing vessel JULIA at that position. Who is calling and why should we change course?"

The heavily accented voice answered, "This is Captain Stanya, we are a fishing boat and we have very long nets out, over 20 miles. We see you on radar and with your current course you will hit our nets and be tangled. Please change your course 40 degrees to port to avoid our nets."

"What if it's a trap?" said Kanek. "What if they're pirates and they're trying to steer us right towards them? No way Skipper, don't change course. It's a trap, I just know it!"

"Oh, I hope there's no trouble," said Ning.

Skip got back on the radio and started a conversation with Captain Stanya asking where he was from, what kind of fish he was catching, how big his boat was, and other questions that only captains of fishing boats could answer with any real knowledge. The back and forth exchange went on for about 10 minutes with Kanek and Ning whispering to themselves in the background. Then Skip asked their opinion, "What do you think guys?"

"Don't alter course," Kanek said with firm resolve.

"Ning?" asked Skip.

"I don't really know. I want to trust them, but it's so suspicious way out here in the ocean. I'd say don't trust them," she replied.

Skip looked at his faithful crew, looked at the charts, stared at the radio, and replied. "Roger Captain Stanya, we are altering course 40 degrees to port. Skip then turned to his crew and said, "I trust him guys. At a certain point, you have to trust people. He sounds honest and I believe him."

Kanek rolled his eyes as he watched Skip throw the helm over hard to port as they changed course. "Oh no, we're done for now," said Ning.

They waited for an hour, all the while scanning the horizon for any sign of a trap. Then, finally they heard the radio again.

It was Captain Stanya calling to say, "Thank you," for changing course because from what he saw on the radar, it appeared as though JULIA had missed the big fishing nets by about ½ mile. He also said, "These are dangerous waters, but I just want you to know that we are not all bad guys." Skip, Kanek, and Ning breathed a big sigh of relief and they got back to their job of sailing JULIA safely on towards Oman.

Later that day, Kanek knocked on Skip's cabin door. "Got a minute?" he asked. Skip nodded and beckoned him in. "Skip, I just want to tell you that I admire you. You made that decision today even though we disagreed with you. If we were voting, we would have won and it would have been the wrong decision. I know you don't trust Ning and me... but we trust you." He turned and walked out of Skip's cabin leaving the captain alone with his thoughts. Making that decision had been difficult, but on a boat there is only one captain and he was it. He had no choice but to act like one.

It was only a day later when Skip managed to connect the boat computer to his email account. Even though the technology to connect from sea existed, it was a long and frustrating process because the information travelled over radio waves bouncing off the atmosphere. It was an old, but tried and true system, and while the messages took minutes to load rather than seconds, it was good to be able to check in with new and old friends. There was an email from Mr. Grey answering their question about whether or not it was okay to mix different oils when adding to the engine. The answer was that it was okay if that's all they had, but not recommended. They got lots of information like that from various sources. "Not recommended" to sail through Pirate Alley, "Not recommended" to go to Oman (unless you were running out of fuel), "Not recommended" to leave to sail around the world when you're a kid...LOL, they laughed about that one!

The third email is what caught Skip's attention. The subject line read, *'URGENT, NING COME HOME.'* Skip called Ning over to the computer, opened the email for her and then left her alone with the message. Skip and Kanek waited and waited for Ning until at last, she came up to the cockpit with tears in her eyes. But they weren't tears of sadness like the boys expected. Through her tears, Ning was smiling

117

and said, "They found him! They found my little brother Piya!" He had been wandering in the hills searching village to village until he finally came to their cousin Sawut's house. Sawut had then travelled to the nearest town to find an Internet café where she emailed Skip's address left by Ning. "Please come home and take care of your little brother," it said. "He needs his big sister."

"Skip, Kanek, as much as I love being with you on this boat, I have to go home. I have to take care of Piya. He needs me…and I need him too. Sawut has even paid for a plane ticket for me. You understand, don't you?"

"Of course we do," the boys said in unison and nodded their heads. "But we'll miss you! We like having you aboard, you're part of the crew! And it's been really good to have a girl onboard!" The boys giggled, and they all hugged. "Maybe you can come back and join us someday," said Skip. "You would sure be welcome!"

Twenty-two days had passed by the time JULIA pulled into the seaport of Odok in the country of Oman. The most striking visual the three sailors noticed were the camels. They were at the port, in the street, some were tied up, some were roaming freely, but there were camels everywhere. And there was oil. Oil tankers, oil refineries, oil trucks, and oil pipelines. That's what struck them: camels and oil.

"Bye! We'll miss you!" shouted Skip and Kanek as Ning walked down the boarding ramp to her plane. It was going to be a long 12-hours with two plane changes in order to get back to Phuket, but as they had all discussed, it was a whole lot faster than the 22 days it took them to get there by sailboat! Ning turned and waved at her friends hoping that someday she would see them again.

During the complicated paperwork to get everybody into Oman safely, the boys began peppering the customs officials with questions about Hina. Had they seen him? Had they heard of him? One of the officials had heard of Hina as evidently he was notorious for having stolen a camel. He had arrived in Odok by stowing away on a freighter carrying copra (coconuts). After stealing a camel, he was thrown in jail and then even the Thai police got involved. It seems that Hina had been living on Phi Phi Phoo beach with a bunch of other kids, and had skipped out on paying the island farmer for the food they had eaten. The long arm of the law reached all the way from Thailand to Oman. But Hina was slippery as a fox and managed to get away while being transferred by car to the courtroom. And nobody had heard from him since then.

They showed Hina's picture all around Odok asking for more information but with no luck until one day, a teenager stopped by the dock and introduced himself as Tibon. He had been Hina's friend while on Phi Phi Phoo beach. Wow, what a wealth of knowledge he had to share! Tibon said he knew exactly where Hina was headed—and why. His next stop was to be Goat Island in the Red Sea, but because the Nami Nami map didn't extend as far as the Red Sea, he no longer was worried about being followed. Tibon said Hina was always angry, always playing tricks on people, and always teasing others. He knew Skip was following him and was leaving him clues just to tease him, but never would allow Skip to find him. He told Tibon he would always be one step ahead of anybody searching for him.

"Why was he going to Goat Island," the boys asked? Tibon wasn't very convincing when he said Hina liked uninhabited places like Goat Island.

"I don't believe you," said Skip. Nobody would travel all that way just to find an uninhabited island. There are plenty of uninhabited places in the world. You're not telling me everything." Tibon shuffled his feet and looked down at the ground, not wanting to make eye contact. Skip and Kanek waited. And waited. And waited. Finally Tibon looked up nervously and whispered, "The treasure."

Skip and Kanek were wide eyed. "The what?!"

"The treasure," Tibon said again. "He's leading you on a wild goose chase because he's such a jerk! He promised me a piece of the treasure if I didn't tell anyone. He told me he would meet me here in Odok and take me with him to find the treasure. But he's a jerk! He was already gone when I got here and I know he's leading you along with false clues because he told me so. He has no intentions of ever letting you catch him. He told me because he was adopted, he doesn't even consider you as his brother and wants no part of you. He's a jerk! Did I say he's a jerk yet? Because he is!" and Tibon sat down hard with his head in his arms.

"Then why was he following the Nami Nami map," asked Skip? "Because that's where the treasure is," Tibon replied. The boys sat down next to Tibon as he spilled everything he knew about Hina. All of this "legend" stuff was getting a little hard to take. "He really was born Boy of the Moon on the island of West Nuku, deep in the South Pacific. Part of the Nami Nami legend of West Nuku is the story of the treasure."

Supposedly, there was indeed a treasure of huge riches in gold and jewels, and those who are born into the role of Nami Nami Protectors, must keep moving to protect it for eternity from thieves. And they leave part of the treasure wherever they see three trees growing in the shape of an "N." "Being born Boy of the Moon, Hina was automatically part of the Protectors. But instead, Hina's a thief, a good for nothing thief!"

"He is not!" Shouted Skip.

"And I'm telling you he is," Tibon shouted back.

"Hey, hey, hey! Calm down!" Kanek jumped between the two boys. "Wait a minute," interrupted Kanek, "Are you saying Hina is one of the Protectors of the treasure?"

"Yes! said Tibon, well, he's supposed to be protecting it. But instead, he's trying to steal it. He's chasing those who are protecting the treasure and whatever they leave buried under the 'N' trees."

Kanek was puzzled. "I still don't understand why he's leaving clues to where he is."

"To throw you off the scent of the trail," Tibon replied. "He's two steps ahead of you, and he always will be."

"No," exclaimed Skip. "He wouldn't do that. He's my brother, my family, he's not a thief, I just know he's not!"

"Look, Skip," Tibon said softly, trying to calm things down. "It's a game of cat and mouse. The real Nami Nami leave him clues to throw him off, he then leaves clues to throw you off. And in the meantime, he's trying to figure out where the Nami Nami are going. What I'm saying is you don't know if the clues were left by Hina or by the real Nami Nami. Let me guess, you didn't by chance go to the island of Kodo, did you?"

Skip and Kanek turned bright furious red and both shouted, "YES! Why?"

"You're lucky then," said Tibon. "You're lucky to be alive because I heard stories of others who weren't so lucky. And Hina didn't care about them. All he cares about is finding the treasure and he thinks if you find him first, you'll somehow be able to stop him." The boys sat back down and thought for awhile. This was a lot to absorb at once. Kanek was the first to speak. "Well Skip, it seems like we have two choices. We can either keep searching for Hina, or we can call it off. I for one, don't want anything to do with the treasure of the Nami Nami. That's theirs and I don't think the Nami Nami warriors are going to treat Hina or anybody else very kindly when they find someone who has been endangering their treasure. Nami Nami law is very strict." Kanek slid his finger across the front of his neck, signifying what was in store for Hina.

Skip sat down at the navigation table and started flipping through the big pile of paper charts. "What are you doing?" asked Kanek.

"We're headed for Goat island," said Skip with such determination in his eyes, that Kanek just nodded.

CHAPTER 15 —PIRATES!

G oat island was in the middle of the Red Sea and to get there, they first had to sail through the notorious part of the Arabian Sea known as Pirate Alley to Yemen.

After refueling JULIA, Skip and Kanek sat down to talk about the upcoming 300-mile passage. "The passage guide says we should stay as far away from shore as possible," read Kanek. "But that we also have to avoid the island of Socotria, a pirate base."

"That course will put us about 80 miles offshore then," said Skip. "No worries for us, we love being far out to sea, right Kanek?"

"Out to sea, out to sea, out to sea," came the voice of Mango from his perch.

"I'm scared," Kanek replied. "What if they shoot at us?"

"Hey, we have weapons too," Skip said. We have flare guns and we have fire extinguishers—remember to shoot right for their eyes with the chemical. We also have pepper spray that would hurt their eyes, and let's not forget our new 'propeller buster.'"

Still, they knew they were no match for pirates armed with machine guns, and were nervous as they departed Odok in the early morning. Once they reached 80 miles out to sea they turned west. As night approached, they were tempted to turn on their running lights but then remembered the rules in pirate waters: No radios or lights that might guide the pirates anywhere close to your position.

It was very early the next morning when Kanek first saw them on the radar. Two small blips approaching very fast from behind. The seas were rough and the winds a blustery 20 knots, and even though JULIA was pounding along at 7 knots, the blips were gaining on them. "Skip! Skip! Wake up!" shouted Kanek. I think we're being followed. Leaping out the aft hatch in one movement, Skip took one look at the radar, one at Kanek, and they both nodded. It was that easy recognition between people who know each other so well; no words needed be spoken, they both knew pirates were chasing them.

Without saying a word, they both leapt into action. Skip went below to break the radio silence while Kanek began readying things in the cockpit. They had practiced this but never thought they would actually need to put their plan into action. "Mayday, mayday, mayday! This is the sailboat JULIA, We are being attacked by pirates!" He repeated it again...and again, but there was no answer on any of the emergency radio channels. He grabbed the satellite phone and dialed the piracy emergency center in London who tracked the positions of all warships in the area. After a minute or so, he hung up the phone. "Bad news" he said to Kanek. The closest ship was a day away, which meant they were on their own. Skip came up to the cockpit carrying a couple of duffle bags, and together he and Kanek opened them and spread out the goods which included the flare guns, pepper spray, and propeller buster.

"Hurry, they're gaining fast," Kanek said after looking at the radar.

The epic battle with pirates!

"Well, let's fix that," said Skip. They unrolled the big billowy genoa, a sail that would normally only be used in lighter wind because of its size. It was risky to fly that sail in strong winds, but when it filled, JULIA took off like a racehorse at nearly 10 knots. They set the autopilot for the fastest route, started the engine, and increased their speed to over 12 knots. At 25 tons, Julia charged through the water like a racehorse and she was steady. She loved this kind of speed and weather. "They're really going to have to work to catch us aren't they?" Kanek said.

"And they'll be tired when they get here," Skip added. "There are two of them, we have to split them up. Let's keep the speed up no matter what; just keep your head down so you don't get shot. When I say "now!" we'll drop over the fishing net propeller buster and that should stop one of the boats completely." Earlier, they had this idea of how to get a pirate's propeller caught in a fishing net. The net had to float, but also had to be sprinkled with metal bars to bend the propeller and jam it. There had been no way to test their invention so they were crossing their fingers that it would work.

"I'll keep firing flares from the flare gun at the other boat which should keep their distance. You take over shooting the flares when I go for the wheel. And then you know what we're going to do." Kanek nodded.

It wasn't long before they could see the two pirate skiffs on the horizon. They were bouncing off the tops of the 5-foot waves and spray was flying everywhere as they pounded into the breaking rollers. When they were about ¼ mile away from JULIA, Kanek and Skip heard the shots. The pirates were firing warning shots at them with machine guns! "Maybe we should just stop and let them take what they want," Kanek said.

"NO!" shouted Skip. "I hate pirates! They're just bullies and I hate bullies. This is going to stop today! No more bullies!"

"No bullies, no bullies, no bullies," squawked Mango. Mango flew out of the main salon and into the cockpit. "No bullies, No bullies," he kept saying. And then suddenly he took flight high into the air and circled the boat from far above. The boys watched as Mango flew to where the pirates were and then tucked into a dive. As fast as a hawk he dove straight for one of the pirate boats. As he swooped down over the pirates, Mango let his big claws out in front of him and slammed right into one of the pirates. He was so quick that he was already on his way back up to the sky before the pirate even knew what had hit him. All the boys could see was the pirate holding his bloody face while he screamed. As Mango circled high above the pirates, Skip and Kanek could hear a loud screeching and squawking of, "No bullies, no bullies, no bullies."

The boys cheered on Mango and now Kanek was fired up too. He began letting out the propeller buster, all 500 feet of it, which wasn't easy to do while trying to keep your head down. Skip loaded the first flare in the flare gun, peeked his head over the rail, aimed at the second boat, and fired. A miss, but the pirates took note and slowed down a bit. Then they sped up again, Skip fired again, another miss. And he fired again, this time a hit right into the center of their boat. They were so close that he could hear a scream come from the pirate boat.

"Look Skip, I think the propeller buster worked!" shouted Kanek. The first pirate boat was stopped, and there were two pirates with their heads over the stern trying to unwrap the net from their outboard motor propeller. Kanek knew that even if they got the net unwrapped, the propeller would be damaged so badly the skiff would only be able to motor about half speed.

Mango saw the stalled boat and went into another fast dive hitting one of the pirates on the behind, knocking him off balance and into the water. The other pirate looking at the motor had enough of "That crazy bird!" He picked up his machine gun and sprayed the sky with bullets. Mango was fast but there were too many bullets. Suddenly there was a loud screeching sound. The boys looked up and could see Mango flying by flapping one wing hard and the other only once in a while to try to keep his balance. He was gliding down and the boys shouted, "C'mon Mango, you can make it! Mango! Here, Mango!" Mango didn't have enough control to land at any one spot with just using a wing and a half. But he was clearly a thinker and flew himself right toward the mainsail. Just as he would have slammed hard into it, he flared up, slowed his speed and hit the mainsail with just a "thud." He then slid down the sail into the cockpit where he limped his way back down into the main salon, blood dripping out of his left wing. He was hobbling around the salon floor in a daze mumbling "No more bullies, No more bullies."

"Mango!" shouted Kanek. "They've hit Mango!" Skip was busy keeping the other boat away by firing flares at them as fast as could load. His aim was getting better by the shot, and after the next one, he could see a small fire erupt on the pirate's boat. The pirate boat stopped. "Give me the flare gun," said Kanek. "Let's finish it."

As they had planned, Skip took the wheel and Kanek kept firing the white-hot flares at the pirates while shouting, "This one's for Mango!" Then Skip turned the wheel hard over, the boys **jibed** the sails, revved the engine to full, and headed straight for the middle of the 25-foot open pirate boat. The pirates were shooting and JULIA was riddled with bullet holes, but before the pirates knew what was happening, JULIA, twice their size and 25 tons, came crashing down in the middle of their boat and split it in two, throwing the pirates into the water.

The first pirate boat with the disabled propeller was almost a mile away now and they still hadn't started their motor. Kanek and Skip thought about going to ram them too, but that would leave them all to drown. And while they hated pirates, they still felt a little bad for them. As Skip looked around at the pirates in the water where their boat was split in half, he saw a few bobbing heads, and shark fins circling the men who were scrambling back up onto the still floating two pieces of hull. At least they weren't going to be eaten but Skip and Kanek both whispered quietly: "No bullies."

Skip and Kanek were so pumped up with adrenalin, and so glad to be alive, they jumped up and down shouting whoops of joy, and headed JULIA back on course for Yemen under full sail and full power. They still had the daylights scared out of them and wanted to get away from Pirate Alley as fast as possible. As the day wore on, the wind picked up, and JULIA seemed to know it was her job to pick up the pace and away she went like a horse racing for the barn. By late afternoon, the radio finally came to life. "Little boat, little boat, little sailing boat, identify yourself." Skip could hardly hold the microphone or see the radio channels through his tears of joy. "Kanek! We're safe. They're here! The coast watch ships are here!" The boys breathed a huge sigh of relief, and as Kanek began bandaging mango, he wouldn't stop talking. "No bullies, No bullies, No bullies…"

CHAPTER 16— WHY THE RED SEA IS BLUE

S kip and Kanek had been nervous about sailing up the red sea. The whole area was so strange to them, it felt even more bizarre than Southeast Asia. Mostly, from what they could see, it was desolate: there was nothing but sand on both shores and as far as they could tell, the hot dry land went on forever. The islands they anchored behind were red and brown. Light red, dark red, light brown, dark brown, bland colors with no vegetation, and the contrast to the lush green south pacific islands was hard to get used to. But it was the contrast that made the journey so interesting. After all, if every place was the same, then, well, everything would be the same and how boring that would be!

As the wind blew hard from the north, they noticed everything on the boat started turning the same reddish/brown color as the desert. The red sand got on the sails turning them a reddish/brown color, it got in the rigging, which they knew was bad because the sand acted like sandpaper rubbing against the metal and weakening it. It got in their hair, there was sand in their food, in their clothes, in their toes, and in their noses, and they laughed because as Kanek said, "It's like living inside a sandbox!"

One day they were anchored behind Sabilia Island and even though they didn't see much of anything or anyone, they decided to go ashore to stretch their legs and walk around. Soon they were pulling their dinghy

129

up onto the sandy shore of the small island and were surprised to hear the tinkling sound of bells. "Sounds like cowbells," laughed Skip.

"Or more like goats?" Kanek said pointing to a place behind Skip.

"Yeah, right, in your dreams," Skip laughed again.

"There you go again, not believing me. I'm not kidding, look!" Kanek said again, this time with his brown eyes nearly popping out of their sockets. Skip turned around slowly and sure enough, there were at least a hundred goats, each wearing a bell, walking along the shoreline. They were followed by a tall bearded man dressed in flowing white robes scooting them along with a stick making a funny sound like "tsk, tsk, tsk." He wore a very long grey beard, and his skin was weather-beaten from the hot dry air and sun. "He looks scary, should we run?" Kanek asked nervously. But the man's long stride brought him too close for them to run and then the boys saw that his smile, which showed just upper teeth remaining, was as wide as the ocean is deep.

Meeting Orin on the Oasis Island in the Blue Red Sea

"Salam, Salam!" said the man. (Hello in Arabic) He could see the boys were a bit frightened so he added "Is okay, is okay!" while he beckoned the boys near. He extended his hand, which held delicious fresh dates. The boys looked at each other, then at the tall smiling man, and while Skip was still suspicious, each took a sweet date.

Skip then put out his hand as a greeting and said, "Friends." The old man smiled broadly, and in quite good English said, "Yes, friends, you and me!" Together they walked to the top of the sand dune where they stopped and stared toward the center of the island. Here on what should have been mere brown barren space, was a lush green Oasis complete with date trees, a fresh water stream fed from deep in the earth, a large green grassy field, and shade palm trees.

Orin talked a lot, as if he hadn't seen anybody in a long time. They learned Orin was an only shepherd on the island who raised and tended to the goats for a village on the mainland. Once a month, a boat came to bring supplies in trade for goats' milk and cheese. Skip kept trying to interrupt to ask all kinds of questions including the name of the island so they could be sure where they were, but Orin was telling a story and Skip had to wait his turn.

They felt bad when they heard his sad story. Orin used to live happily on the island with his wife, son and daughter. But a few years ago, they had all suddenly taken ill and died before the monthly boat arrived to help. To this day, nobody knew what disease, plague, or infection had taken the lives of Orin's family. The only thing different they could come up with was because Orin drank several glasses of goats' milk a day, it must have protected him from succumbing to the same fate. When he offered the boys a glass of goat milk, they eagerly drank it down.

Orin looked sad as he told the story, but said he understood that death was a part of living. The boys knew that only too well and nodded in agreement. The villagers on the mainland had invited Orin to leave the island and live with them, but he liked his remote lifestyle, and had decided to stay and live out his remaining years on the island with his goats.

Skip's patience paid off and he was finally able to get a word in and asked Orin if they were on Sabilia Island? Orin replied that indeed they were, but over the years had taken on the English name, "Goat Island." Skip and Kanek looked at each other, then at Orin, then each other, and back to Orin. Skip blurted out, "Have you seen Hina?" Skip explained who Hina was, and told Orin about the upside down crescent moon on his leg. If they were reading the right clues correctly, and not following the wild goose chase, Hina would have been on Goat Island not all that long ago!

Orin nodded as he spoke. "Yes, I know this boy with the moon on his leg, he was here."

Skip jumped straight up nearly chasing the goats away. "Where is he? Does he live here? Can you take us to him?" Skip had jumped up and was throwing his arms in the air and shouting with glee. The goats just stood and looked at him like he was crazy.

"No, very sorry," Orin said shaking his head. "He is gone. He hitched a ride on a passing fishing boat headed for Egypt. He said he was going to Cairo. He kept saying he was looking for the perfect place." Orin told them about the conversation he had with Hina. "We spoke long into the night about his search and I asked how he would know this perfect place? He said he would know it when he saw it."

"Is there such a place? Will he ever find it?" asked Kanek.

"Yes and no," replied Orin while he pulled on his long white beard. He paused as if to gather his thoughts, touched both hands to his heart and spoke slowly with a voice of wisdom. "There is no perfect place, yet every place is perfect. It is not about seeing the perfection in a place. It is about feeling perfection in one's heart and soul. Then every place can be a perfect place. If you are content, and your heart is filled with love and laughter, and are able to see the beauty all around you, then you have found the perfect place. And it was inside of you all the time—which makes every place a perfect place."

The boys were awestruck. They had never heard such wisdom spoken and didn't even know how to reply. So they just listened and absorbed each word.

"There is something else I must tell you about Hina and what he seeks. This may give you a clue where to look for him."

"Go on," said Skip. He was waiting for Orin to say something about the treasure.

"First, we must eat!" Orin said showing his half-toothed grin. "Always, we must eat together. News is best on a full stomach," he laughed as he led them to a cool place under a big shade tree.

Skip's mood had changed from joy to despair, and now back to curious all in a flash. His head was spinning wildly with thoughts about what Orin was going to tell them. But when he looked at the food Orin was preparing, he suddenly thought of his stomach and agreed! "Okay, let's eat!"

They shared a delicious meal of slow cooked goat meat, three different types of goat cheese, fresh sweet dates, and luscious figs straight from the tree. Skip couldn't stand the suspense anymore. "Please tell us where to look for Hina."

Orin motioned them closer, picked up a small stick and began to draw in the sand. As the drawing became clearer, the boys could make out that it was a map. It had a river, a big city, a big pyramid, and a crescent moon. Orin explained it was indeed a map. He drew it from his memory of once seeing a map belonging to some desert travelers. He explained how the travelers had measured distance by the shape and size of the crescent moon in the upper right corner of each map. The boys looked at each other as their mouths dropped. Their wide eyes revealed what Skip then said, "We know these maps." We have arrived here because of the Nami Nami map, but it ends at the Arabian Sea.

Now it was Orin's turn to be surprised. "You know the Nami Nami map? Then you must learn my friends, the map never ends." One connects to the next and the next so the traveler is never truly lost, and always knows where to go. But I have only drawn your next destination of Cairo. If you miss your brother there, then you will have to have the next map to know where he is going next" You must go to the great Pyramid of Giza. There you will find the next Nami Nami map and the destination of your brother." Orin cautioned them to be careful because the map is considered to be sacred and must not leave its location in the Pyramid. As he spoke, a cold breeze descended on their location and a mini whirlwind kicked up sand and dust. And in an instant, it stopped.

"Did he say anything about treasure?" asked Skip.

"Treasure? What about it?" asked Orin.

Skip hesitated at first, but then started talking really fast and didn't stop until he had told Orin everything he and Kanek had been told about the treasure, and how Hina was looking for it.

Orin listened intently and then spoke softly. "There is no treasure other than peace in life," said the wise man. "I'm afraid it is not something Hina will ever find. He did seem to be in such a hurry to move on. He kept looking at the date trees and how they were growing at different angles. When I asked what he was looking for, he said it was three trees that looked like an 'N,' and asked if there was such a tree formation on the island. That's all he would say, that he had to find the three trees. He seemed so nice at first, but when he left, he took many of my simple possessions. He even took my flashlight!"

It had turned dark and they sat by the side of a fire listening to Orin, asking questions, and then sat in silence. Kanek looked at Skip's big brown eyes that reflected the flames and whispered, "You've gotta be kidding, you're not actually thinking of going into the Pyramid to get that map, are you?" The flames remained in Skip's eyes and he nodded. That was exactly what they were going to do.

Orin asked them to stay for a couple of days to keep him company and the boys agreed. They spent the time listening to Orin's stories, herding goats, and helping with some work hard to do for an old man. It was hot and they sweated, but they were eater to help Orin with his workload.

When it came time to say goodbye, on their last trip ashore, they loaded the dinghy with gifts for Orin. They brought him sacks of food, a new flashlight and batteries, towels, rope, and everything else they felt they could spare and then some. "He needs this stuff more than we do," said Kanek. When they got to the beach, they handed over the overflowing bags they hoped would help Orin live a more comfortable life on the island. *"Shukran, Shukran,"* (thank you in Arabic) said Orin over and over again.

The next morning the boys **weighed anchor** early, just as the sun was coming up over the hot desert. And in spite of the north wind blowing against them, they sailed along steadily north towards Egypt.

CHAPTER 17—
CREEPY PLACES

The sailing was tough and it was slow going as the winds blew steadily against them from the north at 30-40 knots. The strong winds combined with the narrow and relatively shallow Red Sea built the seas up to a huge state. JULIA was pounding into waves the size of 2 and 3-story houses. But they persisted and clawed their way north towards Cairo, in Egypt, 1000 long upwind miles at the north end of the Red Sea.

After nearly two weeks, they were finally able to relax once they had JULIA tied up at the dock in the port of Galeba. They had heard this was the easiest way to get to Cairo and the marina was nice enough that they felt comfortable leaving the boat while they went looking for Hina. They took a local bus to Cairo and then joined a tour headed out to where the Sphinx and the Great Pyramids of Giza sat just as they had for the last 4,000 years. While they were meandering around the biggest of the Pyramids taking photos, an Egyptian boy about their age came up to them and asked, "I am Ahmed and will be your guide. Would you like to go on a special tour inside the Pyramid?"

Skip and Kanek arrange to get inside the Great Pyramid

Skip told Ahmed their story and that they were looking for the Nami Nami map as it would lead them to Hina's next destination. The Egyptian boy's dark eyes opened wide as he shook his head from side to side. He told them it was forbidden to look at the Nami Nami map except by the highest ranked elders.

"Hey, this boy Hina whom you seek, does he have a crescent moon shape birthmark on his right leg?" The boys nodded yes and the Egyptian boy let out a loud sigh of despair. "He caused a big problem, this Hina. He too was looking for the Nami Nami map. He said he just wanted to see it and convinced the elders he meant no harm, and was honest. But when it was in his hands, he ran away with it! There were two and now only one is left so it is kept very safe.

"Where is it?" demanded Skip

Ahmed pointed to the Great Pyramid. "There, inside the King's Tomb at the top of the Great Pyramid."

"We don't want to steal it, just look at it, maybe take a picture of it," Skip said politely.

"That's what your brother said too. If we were caught, the village would ban my family and me forever. No, it's too risky, I'm sorry." They stood in silence for a couple of minutes until Ahmed spoke again. "My family is poor though, and I must provide for them. Perhaps a donation to my family would make it worth taking the risk?" The boys were experiencing a request for Baksheesh for the first time. For thousands of years, Baksheesh has been the custom in this area of the world. It's like a tip, or trading of services for extra money. In this part of the world, it's considered perfectly normal to ask for Baksheesh for giving of services and Ahmed held out his hand indicating he was seeking money. "But we would have to go in at night, after the tourists are gone. And I'm afraid it would have to be a very generous donation to my family."

Skip and Ahmed came to an agreed upon price and sealed the deal with a handshake. "Meet me back here at 10 o'clock tonight!" and in a flash, he was gone.

"Sounds really creepy," said Kanek in a hushed voice. "And I hope he didn't just run off with your money."

139

"He won't. He wants the other half of it and I promised it to him after we see the map."

"Clever, very clever," Kanek offered.

The boys hung out in the tourist areas, ate some BBQ from a local food vendor, and didn't dare ask what they were eating as they suspected it was camel. They took a nap under a big shady palm tree until darkness fell upon them. The Great Pyramid loomed bigger at night as they made their way back toward it and their meeting with Ahmed. It wasn't until 11pm Ahmed came running up to them out of breath explaining he had to wait until everyone was asleep to sneak out of the house. He motioned for the boys to follow him as they approached the huge Pyramid in front of them.

"Is it safe inside?" asked Skip.

"Well, it's been standing for 4,000 years and hasn't collapsed yet," laughed Ahmed.

Now Skip was having second thoughts but Kanek urged him on, reminding him of their mission to find his brother. They entered the huge stone structure though a small tunnel about halfway up the side of the pyramid and Skip immediately felt goose bumps on his arms. "This is really creepy," he said as they crawled up a steep stone ramp on their hands and knees inside a tunnel no taller than half their height. Crawling at a 45 degree angle, their only guide through the darkness was Ahmed's voice, which they followed up, up, up into the deepest darkest center of the Pyramid. Every once in a while Ahmed switched on his flashlight and urged them forward. The light shined bright enough for them to look at the Hieroglyphics carved into the sidewalls of the tunnel. Ahmed explained that the language, which was made up of pictures, showed the life of the king now buried in the tomb where they were headed.

"C'mon Skip, hurry up," whispered Kanek. There was really no reason to whisper, it just seemed like the right thing to do in such a quiet, secret, spooky, creepy place. After about an hour of huffing and puffing their way up the stone tunnel, they could feel the air was less damp and somewhat warmer, and then suddenly, they were able to stand. They were in the innermost burial chamber of the pyramid, and right in front of them was the King of Egypt who ruled over 4,000 years ago. Ahmed explained the room they were in was located in the middle of the pyramid and nearly at the top. That meant they were about 200 feet in, and nearly 400 feet up, inside the giant stone structure. The marble **sarcophagus** in which the King had been entombed was enormous, about 10 feet long and five feet wide, and it was covered with inscribed pictures. Ahmed showed them how to read some of the Hieroglyphics and from what they could make out, the story showed a king rich with gold and treasure. He had lots of poor people working for him in the fields, but he then died at a pretty young age. "Maybe if he had shared more of his riches with the farmers in the fields, he might have lived longer," Kanek said in a snarky tone.

"It does seem a shame that one person had so much and the workers had so little," added Skip. "I wonder why he didn't just give the riches to all the people? I bet he never got that good feeling you get from giving. Heck, we just give batteries and t-shirts to people, and that makes us feel good!" Ahmed pointed out many rulers in countries all over the world kept the people poor by selfishly keeping the riches of the country for themselves. "I guess so," Skip said, "but that doesn't make it right." All of the boys nodded in agreement. Just then a blast of hot air seemed to envelop the room and the boys all got a funny feeling in their stomachs. "Where is the Nami Nami? Asked Skip.

Ahmed pointed to a smaller marble sarcophagus. "In there. C'mon give me a hand, the cover is heavy!" They pushed and shoved but only could move the heavy marble cover an inch at a time. "Keep pushing!" and the boys finally moved the cover enough to see inside. There, in the bottom, was a gold tube. And next to the tube was Skip's worst nightmare, a coiled up Cobra ready to strike!

"Oh no, I'm outta here," said Skip. No way am I reaching in there! "C'mon, Let's get out of here. It's not worth it. Hina is on his own, this place is giving me the creeps!"

"Wait! I have an idea." Ahmed grabbed Skip's arm. "You said you were going to take a picture of the map, right?" Skip nodded. "The flash from your camera will blind the snake just long enough for me to reach in and grab the tube."

Skip was starting to feel dizzy. Kanek helped him sit down away from the snake and took the camera from him. "I'll do it," Kanek said bravely.

"Okay, on the count of three, you shoot the flash and I'll reach in. But then we must get the cover back on quickly. Can you help us Skip?"

Unsure of where he was getting his strength from, Skip got up and came around behind the mini sarcophagus, leaned his weight onto the cover and said, "Ready to push!"

"One, two, three!" Kanek clicked the flash blinding the snake just long enough for Ahmed to reach in and grab the tube. And just as the snake recovered and was ready to chase after the tube, Skip leaned all his weight against the lid and shoved it back over the tomb locking the snake back inside. "Got it!" shouted Ahmed.

The boys spread the map out on top of the king's tomb and sure enough, it was a Nami Nami map and had the crescent moon legend just like the other Nami Nami map. Skip took photo after photo, had Kanek put his hand down next to the crescent moon so they would know its size later, and then called out that he was done.

The boys looked at each other. "Oh no…are you kidding me?" moaned Skip. "We have to put it back?" Ahmed nodded and so the boys took up their positions at the small tomb. They could hear the snake hissing inside. "I don't think this is going to be as easy, the snake is onto us."

Just then, the boys heard a high pitched squeal from the corner of the tomb. Ahmed shined the flashlight and they saw a small rat in the corner. That gave him another idea. He told Kanek to do the same camera flash trick on the rat so he could catch it. "Then we'll throw the rat into the snake to distract it. He must be hungry!" It worked. Ahmed caught the rat, Kanek moved the lid just enough to drop it in for the snake's meal, and they dropped the map in its tube back into the tomb. Skip shoved the lid back and sealed the marble top. And then without any warning, Skip tossed his cookies right there on the floor of the tomb. "Ugh, I'm sorry guys, but we just threw that rat to its end. And all because of Hina. He's starting to make me mad!"

They were all sweating and Skip's nerves were clearly rattled. "Now let's get out of here!" and they all couldn't wait to get back to the tunnel. "How do we get down?" Skip was starting to get really frazzled by the creepiness coming over him.

"Like this!" shouted Ahmed as he laid down on his backside on the smooth stone, crossed his hands over his stomach, and shoved off. Aaaahhhhhhhaaaaayaaaaahoooo!"

"No thanks, I'll crawl backwards," Skip said without hesitation. "Call me a coward or whatever, but I'll be down in a while."

"Okay, see you at the bottom," said Kanek and whoosh! Off he went sliding down the dark tunnel. He and Ahmed waited until Skip finally joined them after his slow crawl down. He'd had enough excitement for the night.

When they finally got to the tunnel entrance, they could feel the cool night air warming up and could see light on the horizon as the sun was about to rise. They climbed down the side of the Great Pyramid just before the first tourists arrived. Once they were back to the ground, Skip and Ahmed finished their business deal and the boys said their goodbyes. Skip and Kanek headed toward the bus station and Skip said, "We have to find a place to print these pictures. Then we can piece them together and make our own Nami Nami map. But where? It's not like there's a print shop on every corner." While the boys were walking away from the Pyramids, the tourists were starting to arrive—and so were the street vendors who were selling everything from mini-Pyramids to post cards. One man they saw was wearing a sign that said, "Your Photo with the Pyramids in Print Right Now!" He was short and rather pudgy and had leathery skin from being in the hot sun his whole life. He had a new printer hanging in front of his stomach from two shoulder straps and a harness. Actually, his stomach did a good portion of the work of holding the printer in place. On his back, he wore a battery pack to power the printer.

"Excuse me Mister," said Skip. "We would like to rent your printer. We would like to print about 20 pictures."

"Oh, I could never do that, that would use too much printer ink," the man said as he turned to walk away.

Skip followed him and got him to stop and listen once more by saying one word; "Baksheesh!" As the man turned around, Skip said, "Perhaps a donation to your family would allow you to buy more ink?" The man smiled. They struck a deal and began printing the pictures at the one-man print shop right there in the desert. It was indeed an odd sight and Skip and Kanek couldn't help but laugh at where they were and what they were doing. It was all of their anxious nerves formed into laughter and they were glad to ease the tension from the night before.

Back at the boat, printed pages in hand, the boys spread the pieces of the puzzle out on the salon floor and began taping them together. In between shooing Mango away, slowly the map came into view. It covered a big portion of the world, showing Egypt, the Mediterranean Sea, and parts of the Atlantic Ocean. It showed the sailing routes followed by ancient traders, and included drawings of gold coins in Spain, Morocco, and the Spanish Islands of the Canaries. It also showed the skull and crossbones, the symbol for pirates there. They stared in awe at the map they had constructed and eventually Skip said, "Well, let's see where the crescent moon took Hina." Mango sat on Kanek's shoulder and repeated, "Hina, Hina, Hina, cracker, cracker, cracker, Mango, Mango, Mango."

They used Kanek's hand as the measurement again and when he lifted his hand off the map, they could see a tiny island surrounded by a dotted line indicating it was often underwater. They could just barely read the one word—'Elanti.' Skip let out a low whistle. Kanek listened intently as Skip told him the story of the lost city of Elanti in the Greek Islands. He explained what he had heard and read; that the city of Elanti was buried during a huge volcanic eruption. The earthquake that followed sunk the whole place and the entire city was now under water. Some rumors said the city was so well built that it's buildings were waterproof and there was an entire population still living in the city under the water! "Hina sure likes weird places, doesn't he?"

"As long as there's a volcano nearby," said Kanek. "I guess he only went to Egypt to get his own Nami Nami map so he would know where to go next! I guess we're headed for the lost city of Elanti and maybe we'll find out," said Kanek.

"Elanti, Elanti, Elanti, we're headed for Elanti," squawked Mango.

From Galeb, they sailed to the Suez Canal and before they knew it, were motoring through what seemed like the most enormous ditch ever dug in the world. Which in fact, it was! It took two days to transit the entire 120 mile canal and at the end of that second day, JULIA popped out into the very blue, cool Mediterranean Sea.

CHAPTER 18 — THE UNDERWATER CITY

It was only a 2-day sail to the first of the Greek Islands and by this time, the boys' skills had improved so much, they sailed the boat with true teamwork. And it seemed as luck was on their side as they made the sail with no breakdowns of equipment!

The only problem was when they reached the point where the island of Elanti should have been, all they saw was a small and narrow strip of reef and sand no more than a mile long and half that in width, and most of it was underwater. They sailed around it a couple of times and then used the depth sounder to find an anchorage shallow enough on the protected side of the island to drop JULIA's heavy anchor and chain. Then they just looked at each other wondering what to do next. "Where's the city?" asked Kanek.

"Heck if I know," Skip replied. "I told you everything I know about the place, and it's all just rumors. It is high tide though, maybe something will become more visible when the tide goes out." Six hours later, when the tide had retreated, the sandy island was still only a foot or two out of the water. It seemed if there was an underwater city of Elantis though, they weren't going to find it sitting on the boat. "I guess it's down there," Skip said pointing down toward the water. "C'mon, let's get the scuba gear ready. Remember, we're here to find a clue where Hina

145

might be, so keep your eyes open." Before their dive, they reviewed the most common hand signals used to communicate underwater. Thumb down to descend, thumb up to surface, thumb and index finger forming a circle for OK, hands crossed in an X to abort the dive, and a few others. The boys had learned communication on the boat was the key to safety and super important in getting along with each other. Underwater, it was even more crucial they understand each other. And they agreed to follow the most important rule of never letting the other person out of their sight. Putting all of their gear on was a cumbersome process and they had to help each other with wet suits, vests, weight belts, air tanks, knives, compass, watch, flashlights, flippers, and masks. Then they double checked their air gauges, gave each other the "OK" sign, and holding their masks, jumped into the clear blue water. Floating on the surface, they once more gave the "OK" sign, and then thumbs down to dive. As they slowly let the air out of their vests, the weight belts pushed them down 10 feet, 20 feet, 30 feet, and then 40 feet where they added a little air back into their vests and leveled off. The boys floated effortlessly in the clear deep blue water as if they were weightless in space, spinning around and around, but all they could see were big rock formations. There certainly was no sign of a city. Skip said with hand signing for them to swim in a direction parallel to the strip of land but after swimming for 20 minutes, he signaled it was time to turn around and head back to the boat. He figured another 20 minutes to swim back plus a little spare air, so it was time to turn around. Disappointed, they swam back to their point of entry, surfaced, and climbed back aboard JULIA. The diving was uneventful this time, but the boys were still exhausted. They weren't used to all of that exercise. "Tomorrow will be another day," said Skip.

And indeed it was. The boys were up early and rowed the dinghy to shore to explore the thin strip of land. They were looking for any clue to the whereabouts of the lost city of Elantis but there wasn't a boat, car, house, or even a tree on the barren sandy strip. There was something odd though. Further down the beach, they began seeing what looked like brown clay pots scattered all around them. Kanek bent over to pick one up but it wouldn't budge. As he wrestled with it, he realized it wasn't a pot after all; it was a tube and it went straight down into the ground. It had a cover that popped up and down two inches as if to seal the tube. The boys went to another tube and saw that it too headed into the ground. There was cool air coming out of all of the tubes. "They're air shafts!" shouted Skip. "This is how they get air. I bet the city is right underneath us!"

"Oh yeah? If there's a city underneath here, how do they get in?" asked Kanek.

"Good question." said Skip and they both sat down in the sand to think. "Tomorrow let's move the boat down here to this end of the beach and we'll dive in this area. Maybe we'll find the answer then."

Another early day began with moving JULIA a half mile and re-anchoring her securely. Then they used the air compressor to re-fill the dive tanks, got all of their gear ready, but then admitted they were too tired to dive right away. A rest and a peanut butter and jelly sandwich picked up their energy and soon the boys were jumping over the side back into the blue water.

They didn't have to swim far before they saw what looked like a black hole with air bubbles coming out of it. Lava tubes are formed when hot lava is draining out of a volcano. As the lava cools, the drain, which is essentially a naturally formed pipe, hardens into a tube. Skip saw the bubbles coming out of this lava tube entrance and realized it was wide enough to swim into with their scuba gear. It's dangerous because some tubes get too narrow to turn around in, but Skip was determined, and fear was a thing of the past for him. And while he wouldn't admit it out loud, he was privately getting tired of being one or even two steps behind Hina. It was as if this was his last effort to find him. Kanek, having great faith in his friend, followed close behind.

They swam straight down into the 3-foot wide lava tube, followed it to the right, then left, then down some more, then horizontal, and finally, upwards they swam. Skip noted on his depth gauge they were about the same depth as when they entered the tube. As they leveled off, they saw light ahead, swam a bit farther and then popped up into air. Fresh, clean air! They found themselves in a blue-green pool and as they took their scuba air regulators out of their mouths, and spun around taking in the scene, they couldn't believe their eyes. They were in a giant cavern. There were beautiful carvings in the rock walls of a real ancient city. The carvings, like the Egyptian hieroglyphics they had studied before, showed plazas, large stone buildings, doors to houses and shops, and farmers bringing gifts of food to a king and queen sitting in a throne. Hanging down from the top of the giant cavern's ceiling were dozens of tubes: "The air tubes from above!" whispered Kanek.

They swam to the rock edge and and discovered steps carved into the rock, as if it were a swimming pool. As they made their way out of the water they heard noises like the sound of someone shuffling along, dragging their feet. The boys stopped and stared as a small man, or creature, or fish, or man-fish slowly came out from behind a large rock. It had big wide round fish-like eyes. But on the side of its face where its cheeks would be, this creature had gills just like a fish. It had a big wide mouth and fat lips and tiny ears. It was short, about four and a half feet tall, with light green rough looking skin that resembled fish scales. The man-fish stood on two legs and had webbing between its toes on its feet.

Skip and Kanek meet the man-fish, Dorkus

The boys didn't move or speak and for about a minute, the three of them stood still looking each other over trying to sense if the other was friend or enemy. The man-fish spoke first in perfect English with a British accent. "Who are you and why are you here?"

Surprised to hear the creature speak English, Skip stammered and stuttered, Uh, um, we, um, well, we're here because, well, actually, where are we? Where is here? Oh, and uh, well, I'm Skip and this is my friend Kanek, and we're looking for my long lost brother Hina, and…"

"Is this going to be a long story?" asked the man-fish while rolling his big eyes. "I was just about to have lunch and now I have to listen to your long story? Come, join me for lunch. We're having seaweed, sea-rice, and my favorite, green algae with extra slime." The boys looked at each other and Skip whispered, "Eww, barf!"

"I heard that. Just because my ears are small doesn't mean I can't hear. In fact, I hear about 100 times better than humans and I can hear through water."

"Oops, sorry," Skip apologized. "Excuse me for asking, but *what* are you? Are you a fish or a human?" The boys followed the man-fish along a wet slimy rock path that stopped in front of a huge boulder 3 times their height. The man-fish made a gurgling noise that sounded like bubbles and almost immediately the boulder rolled to the side revealing a much larger cavern where at least 100 more of the man-fish creatures were seated on giant snail shells at tables made of huge clamshells. It was loud from all of the chattering which was a mixture of English and gurgling, and it sounded like everyone was trying to talk to each other underwater. There were huge seaweed plants growing down from the ceiling and others growing up from the cavern floor. It was brightly lit and the air was fresh, all from the air tubes the boys had discovered. Seawater splashed at their feet and as they followed their guide, the room fell silent. In gurgling English, he introduced the boys as friends and that seemed good enough for the crowd who went back to their chatter.

As they sat down at a clamshell table, plates of food were placed in front of them piled high with food from the sea. Kanek was the first to taste it, and from the way he began devouring the meal, Skip could tell he liked it. "Yum! May I please have some more algae with extra slime?" asked Kanek. At that, Skip pinched his nose and took his first bites. Then he too ate until he could eat no more. He just nodded as Kanek said, "This is what I call real SEAfood!"

They finished their meal but were getting a bit nervous as the water-level in the cavern was slowly rising and was now past their ankles. Their host, the man-fish explained it was the rising tide but they had nothing to worry about as that was as high as it would go...usually... and the air vents had tops that close under the pressure of water when the ride rises. He then let out a huge belly laugh and burp. "Aaaahhhhh," he sat back, relaxed, and before you could say 'seaweed,' was snoring away sound asleep. The boys looked at each other with wide eyes recognizing what a very strange place they were in. They didn't have to speak as they both were already thinking of how to get out.

Just then, a large drop of water from the ceiling landed right in the big right eye of the man-fish and he woke with a start. "Ahem, yes, now where was I. Oh yes, I was telling you about my people." The boys nodded their heads and he continued. "We are all that is left from the lost city of Elantis. I am Dorkus, the oldest and they say, the wise one. I've lost count, but I think I am 1,239 years old, born well after the sinking. You see, when the volcano erupted, it caused an earthquake and the entire city sank about 60 feet underwater. Most of the people drowned but this area was left in an air pocket only 30 feet below the surface and a few hundred survived. There was no way out so they created the air tubes you see here. That of course, was over 2,000 years ago and to survive, our bodies evolved over hundreds of years and many generations, as we spent more and more time in the water. We developed gills so we can breathe air and we can also get some of our oxygen from the water. It's really quite convenient! We are becoming aquafied and the youngest generation can actually live in the water like fish. We have heard that scientists call us Piscus Sapiens, those that believe we are here that is."

"Do you have enough food? What about water?" asked Skip.

"Plenty of food, yes we have," said Dorkus. We have discovered new ways of farming kelp and seaweed, we have built fish farms, we harvest algae, and we have developed sea-rice made from ground up snail and lobster shells. It's very high in protein and our healthy diet has stopped us from dying off. We make fresh water by filtering the salt water through the ground up shells and in fact, our population is now remaining steady."

"Don't you want to come back to the surface?" asked Kanek?

"What for?" replied Dorkus. "To have the troubles we hear so much about? To chase physical possessions? To have war and famine and poverty? No thank you, we are quite happy right where we are. We have the entire ocean to explore and future generations will prove it was a mistake for fish to come out of the water to land in the first place."

This was a lot for the boys to take in. At first, it was unbelievable but there they were, talking to Dorkus and it wasn't a dream.

"Now tell me why you sought to find us? We have very few visitors and the ones who have found us, have never left. Oh, not because we ate them, they just decided to stay. Although we could have eaten them…" Dorkus said while licking his lips with his big tongue as his big eyes rolled back in his head.

"Hey!" shouted Skip. "Cut it out!"

"Oh yes, so sorry, I do get carried away at times. It's been so long since I tasted meat…," he drifted off again, his eyes rolling back in his head and his tongue smacking his lips. Then in an instant, he was back again. "So, tell me again why you are here."

"We're looking for my long lost brother, Hina. He ran away from home years ago and we've been sailing all the way around the world looking for him," said Skip. He went on to explain how his mother had died and left him Brian's last post card from Tahiti, how he had a crescent moon birth mark, and…"

Dorkus interrupted, "Did you say a crescent moon birthmark? On his leg?" Skip and Kanek nodded. "Yes, we saw him wandering around on the surface for two days in a row. Just about a month ago. We could see him through the tubes and we noticed his unusual birthmark. But there is only one way in or out and you found it, he did not."

Skip was excited now. "Do you know where he went?" he asked.

"No idea," answered Dorkus. "But tell me, young man, why do you seek him?"

"Because he's my brother, he's my only family. We're brothers and I'm sure he wants to be with me again!"

"You say he is lost?" asked Dorkus. Skip nodded.

"Are you sure he is the lost one?" Dorkus said very slowly. As he looked up, he could see tears running down Skip's cheeks. "And ponder this young one, does he want to be found?"

"If I find him, then I will have my family again," said Skip.

"Really? What will he provide for you don't already have? Because it looks to me as though you already have a family," Dorkus said with great wisdom. "Is he not your brother?" He pointed his webbed fingers toward Kanek.

The boys listened intently as Dorkus poured out his hundreds of years of wisdom. "Your life is YOUR life, and your happiness does not depend on finding Hina. Your happiness depends on how you live your life. Do not look outward for love and satisfaction, look inward at your own heart. When you love yourself, when you are satisfied with yourself, then you will attract the love and family you need and want. Then I am confident Hina will find you. Because from what you tell me, if he wanted to be found, he would have let it happen. Have you considered he doesn't feel the same about you?"

"Why don't you stay with us?" asked Dorkus. "We can eat you, I mean, eat together..." and his voice trailed off as he once again licked his lips with his giant tongue and his eyes rolled back into his head.

Kanek and Skip looked warily at each other and Kanek said, "We have to go now, it's getting late." As they donned their scuba gear, the boys noticed there were four other Piscus sapiens getting ready to get in the water with them. They looked like Dorkus but each had four large fangs protruding outside their mouths.

"My guards will escort you," said Dorkus, as his eyes rolled back in his head and his big tongue licked his lips....

"That's okay, we can find it ourselves," said Skip.

"Oh, I insist," mumbled Dorkus, his tongue now hanging out of his mouth. "But my guards are so large at the hip, they can't fit through the tube. They will take another route, too dangerous for you, and meet you at the end of the tube. We wouldn't want anything to happen to you, would we?" His eyes and tongue now rolling around, and his tongue slapping back and forth across his mouth.

"Oh, you know, I forgot my watch. It's in the dining room," said Skip. "Could you get it for me?" he asked Dorkus.

"Mmmm, okay, I'll be right back." As Dorkus turned to walk away, Skip and Kanek used their agreed upon sign language to indicate, "Let's Go!" and they quietly slipped into the water, found the tube entrance and swam as fast as they could. Behind them, they could hear loud noises, like the clanging of an alarm. Then they heard splashes, one, two, three, four and they knew the four "guards" were behind them. They had figured out that while Dorkus may have been wise in knowledge, he was hungry for the taste of meat! The boys kicked their flippers as hard as they could, and pulled themselves along the tube. They were safe inside the tube because the guards couldn't fit in there, but what were they going to do once they reached the end? They didn't know, but still kicked and pulled their way as fast as they could until they could see the end of the tube. And there, staring at them were the big eyes of the guards! Their fangs were now shining bright, and their tongues were slapping back and forth along their lips. Their eyes were rolling back in their heads just like Dorkus and the boys knew they were the colony's next delicacy to be served on a clamshell table! They were trapped. Back into the hands of Dorkus or forward into his guards who would bring them back to Dorkus. The boys looked at each other and gave the signal for "I don't know what to do!"

Then it happened. The boys heard a splash louder than they had ever heard and the resulting wave was so strong, they had to hold onto the sides of the tube. As they looked out the end of the tube, they saw the first guard hit from the side by what looked like a huge black and white monster. The guard was hit so hard, its body just hung limp in the water and then began to sink. The next guard took its position and then it was hit on the other side, this time by an enormous grey and white body. The boys watched in awe as the last two guards struggled to hold their position at the end of the lava tube. But like the others, they were both soon sinking to the bottom. The next thing the boys saw was an enormous eye looking at them. The eye was of a giant Orca and it was twitching. Circling around on patrol was an enormous dolphin with three white scratch marks on its left cheek. The boys were almost screaming with joy as they flung themselves out of the tube, grabbed hold of the giant Orca's dorsal fin and let it carry them straight back to the boat so fast they could barely hold on! All the while, the huge dolphin circled and nodded its head in approval. Skip's heart skipped a beat and he became so dizzy, he nearly lost his grip on the Orca. Kanek reached over and grabbed his arm to help him hold on.

Within about two minutes, they were at the swim ladder of JULIA and were ready to climb aboard. But instead, they stayed in the water and swam around playing with the Orca and Bottlenose dolphin. For this time, the boys surely knew who they were with, as Kanek could feel the strength of his grandfather, and Skip heard a voice in his head, "Remember Skip, I will be there when you need me."

CHAPTER 19—THE BIG DECISION

After their mysterious experience with the giant Orca and Bottlenose dolphin, Skip and Kanek had no choice but to change what they believed to be true and possible. It seemed as though as long as they were at sea, they would be protected by Kanek's grandfather and Skip's mother. "I don't know what to believe anymore, said Skip.

"It seems pretty clear to me," said Kanek. The great spirits have rescued us again but we can't go on depending on them for our whole lives. And Skip, I know this is going to be hard to hear, but is Hina worth it? Maybe he doesn't want us to find him. And if we do find him then what? Do we kidnap him and make us sail with us? We, and especially you, have some thinking to do. And Skip, I have to say this. I want to support you, and I hope someday everything works out and you find Hina, but…well, I think in the quest to find Hina, one or both of us is going to lose our life. And even if not, you're going to lose me in the process.

"I don't care about you then!" Shouted Skip! "NO! I'm not giving up on Hina!"

Kanek burst into tears when he heard that. He pleaded with his friend, "Skip! You are not responsible for Hina! We've almost died more than once searching for him and he just leads us on a wild goose chase. You may as well be chasing the moon as you are the Boy of the Moon!"

That made Skip furious. They were at a calm anchorage and there wasn't a breath of wind. It was hot and Skip was sweating and turning red with anger and frustration. He went to the base of the mast and started climbing. Step by step, holding onto the rigging and pulling himself up, up, up until he was at the very top of the mast. Then he just hung on there as the mast swayed back and forth with the light rolling of the boat. Kanek ignored him and went to work on boat projects. Skip watched from high above as Kanek began polishing the stainless steel on the rails. Occasionally he would head below to the galley and was clearly cooking up something delicious as the warm smells of vegetables, beef, olive oil and pasta wafted up to Skip's perch. Skip's mind was racing. He looked far off to the horizon wondering what Hina was really like and why he didn't want to be with Skip as family. Then he looked down at Kanek polishing, cooking, and working to make the boat as much of a home as possible. What more could Skip want in a brother than he already had? Skip wasn't able to control what came next and he was overwhelmed by a flood of tears. His arms were getting tired and he let himself down to the deck carefully step by step and surprised Kanek down below in the galley.

Kanek could see Skip was upset and sat down to listen. "Even though Dorkus wanted to eat us, I wonder if you and Dorkus are right? I think he meant well, but he just couldn't help himself. He said he hadn't eat meat in about 1,000 years, so I guess I understand that he couldn't control himself. I think I can forgive him for trying. Maybe we should focus on what he said, and what you're saying Kanek. Orin said it, Dorkus said it, and between them there's a lot of years of wisdom. And now you're saying it. Maybe we should stop chasing Hina. He knows we've been trying to find him, and he obviously isn't ready to be found. Why else would he keep moving instead of stopping and waiting for us? Then again, he wants to find that treasure, but we don't care about it." Skip was filled with questions and the boys talked long into the night about their options.

"I don't want to give up," Skip said. "I'm not a quitter. On the other hand, I don't like that Hina is chasing a treasure to steal. I don't think I want to be associated with his kind. He's who I sailed away from, why am I so eager to find a bully? But I would have to go against my mom's wishes...."

"Your mom had no way of knowing how Hina turned out. My grand-father used to say you can't control everything Skip. Events and circumstances happen. He also told me the only thing you can control is how you react to what happens. I know you're frustrated and disappointed, but maybe we should just enjoy our own lives and not worry about Hina's. And maybe we should just count our lucky stars that we're alive and see what's out there waiting for us. Hina will find you when and if he's ready, and then we'll all be family. We could even go back to Thailand and ask Ning and her brother Piya to join our family too."

"Ohhhh, you liked her. Kanek likes Ning!"

"Do not!" shouted Kanek

"Do too! Kanek has a girlfriend!"

Mango added, "Kanek has a girlfriend!" and that made Skip struggle not to smile. "Well, we're a long ways from Thailand so I hope you're patient," said Skip. He was exhausted from the whole thinking process and the effort it was taking to let go of his dream of finding Hina. He laid down quietly, looking sad, closed his eyes and fell fast asleep. In his dreams, Skip saw dolphins everywhere and one in particular—the giant Bottlenose Dolphin with the three white scratch marks on its side. *'Talk to me mom,'* he whispered in his dreams. *'I don't want to be a quitter, but I don't think Hina wants to be found.'*

When he woke up the next morning, Skip told Kanek about his dreams. "And what did your mom say to you?" Kanek asked eagerly.

"She told me I should follow my heart. That's all, just follow my heart. I think following my heart means being content for now." Skip was careful with his words and repeated, "For now. I'm not saying I'm quitting, or giving up, but it does seem Hina's been kind of a jerk." He paused and let that sink in. "I can't believe I just said that." They discovered a new sense of contentment now that they weren't looking for Hina. They could just let life unfold as it happened. Hopping from island to island, from one picturesque anchorage to the other, they slowly sailed west—always west...Italy, France, and Spain all became temporary homes as they made their way across the Mediterranean Sea. They learned to say, "Yes, no, please, thank you," and "where is the bathroom," in Arabic, Hebrew, Turkish, Greek, Italian, French, and Spanish.

"This is the last port in the Med (the short name for the Mediterranean) and speaking Spanish means we're at the end of the line," Skip said one morning. "You see that narrow-looking channel? That my friend is the Strait of Gibraltar." While the channel may have looked narrow, it was actually eight miles across, and outside the channel was nothing but ocean—a big blue ocean. Now it was time to get down to some serious planning, as they faced crossing the mighty Atlantic Ocean. There would be no rest stop, no assistance for a distance of nearly 3,000 miles.

The boys' first order of business was to make sure all vital systems onboard JULIA were in good working order. They reviewed page after page of to-do lists and used the A,B,C,D priority system Mr. Grey had taught Skip. Everything ended up on one list or another.

So they set out to tackle the "A" list. Replacing the engine alternator was number one on the list and they spent two full days before they actually found one that would fit JULIA's engine. They bought two, one to take along as a spare, and sealed it in a waterproof plastic bag.

They crossed things off the "B" list fairly quickly because they were mostly small tasks such as replacing the **chafe gear** on many of the lines. This was thick leather or canvas that prevented the lines from wearing through in one place from continued use, and it was a never-ending but important job.

Items on the "C" list were also easily accomplished as they included hiking up to the top of the Rock of Gibraltar to see the view and the monkeys. The monkeys had been in Gibraltar for centuries and hundreds of them roamed freely about the mountain. Upon reaching the summit, Skip and Kanek wandered the trails with the other tourists. Mango had followed them and was circling overhead calling out, "Candy bar, Candy Bar." Kanek was munching on a candy bar and they stopped to look at a cute monkey with his big brown eyes and adorable face. Before Kanek even knew what was happening, the monkey reached out with lightning speed, grabbed the candy bar and raced off into the bushes. "Hey! Come back here!" shouted Kanek, but it was too late. As he turned to get Skip's sympathy, he saw his best friend on the ground rolling around in hysterical laughter at the monkey's antics. "It's easy for you to laugh, it wasn't your candy bar!" Kanek said. From overhead, Mango screeched, "Watch the monkey, watch the monkey!"

Kanek loses his candy bar to the monkeys of Gibraltar

"Oh, that was so funny, you should've seen your face!" Skip said. "Here, you can have mine, it was worth it just to see how fast that monkey was!"

Food provisioning was next and by the time they were done with their purchases, they had wheeled four shopping carts out of the market and were loading all of the food into every storage area, cupboard, and small space available, Kanek asked, "Hey where do the potatoes go?"

"Oh, you can put them anywhere," Skip said.

Kanek answered with a big grin, "Sorry, anywhere is full!" and they laughed out loud as they often did when one of them said this. The laughter made any job go quicker and easier.

CHAPTER 20—A NEW CLUE

"**I**s that it? Have we done everything on our "A" list? Have we done everything we can to make this passage a safe one?" Skip asked himself out loud and answered his own question, "Yes, we have. Well then, Let's go!" He still had butterflies in his stomach though, as he did every time they went to sea.

"Kanek, cast off the dock lines, we're headed to sea!" Skip loved saying that. It made him feel so free and independent. He felt like he was indeed, the master of his fate, the captain of his own life. As they motored out of the marina toward the Strait of Gibraltar, they both waved goodbye to friends on the dock, and then stared in silence at the ocean that awaited its newest visitor.

"I've never seen seas this big!" Kanek said as he handed Skip his harness and short tether so they would both be tied to the boat. The weather was calm, nice easy winds and clear skies, but the huge swells were coming from far up in the north and were rolling along under them like rising and falling hills. JULIA surfed down the faces of the swells with great ease and the autopilot was working without any problems. The giant swell would pick up the stern as if getting the boat ready, and then launch her screaming down the face of the wave. When she reached the trough, the boat would slow down as the rest of the swell rolled under her. Then the next swell would come along, pick up her stern, and off they'd go again. After a few days of this, the boys were actually getting used to living in the roller coaster ride they called home.

163

Going this fast improved their odds at fishing. Nearly every day they caught either a delicious mahi-mahi or yellow fin tuna. One day, they caught an enormous tuna that was longer than they were tall! They had enough fresh fish to eat like kings every day. After they caught a fish though, they brought in their fishing lines because as Kanek had taught Skip about the lobsters in Vanuatu, they didn't want to catch more than they could eat. The ocean and its fish were their co-inhabitants, kind of like roommates. They didn't want to kill anything unless it was for eating purposes.

Their speed and big bow wave gave the dolphins a new play area. At least twice a day a pod of dolphins could be seen jumping, leaping, flipping, rolling, and surfing just off the bow of the boat. The boys would run up to the boat and shout encouragement like, "Yahoo!" and "Go Dolphins, Go!" It seemed they heard the boys, for when they shouted, the dolphins jumped higher and did more tricks. Skip always looked for that one big bottlenose dolphin with three white streaks on its side, and occasionally he saw it. But it seemed the dolphin and Orca were letting go, showing up less often, and giving the boys back the responsibility for their own lives.

Dolphins surfed with them for 3,000 Miles Across the Atlantic Ocean

It wasn't always exciting but as Kanek said one day, "A boring passage is a good one. It means that nothing has broken!" They read lots of books, repaired little things, trimmed the sails, cooked, cleaned the boat every day, and sailed on day after day on an ocean that seemed to go on forever. Most of the days they traveled about 160 miles, and on their fastest day, they covered 200 miles. After 12 days, Skip said, "Only one more week to go and we'll reach the Caribbean." And they both faked a "Yahoo!," for what they had discovered is they liked being at sea. This felt like home to them. What they hadn't talked much about was the impending end of their journey. If they weren't searching for Hina anymore, then what were they doing sailing around the world? There was the adventure, it was a given they enjoyed the challenge and exploration of remote places only a boat could lead them to. They even knew they enjoyed the dangerous places they had visited and the quest to find Hina had certainly provided them purpose for their journey. Without that purpose, they seemed lost.

Nothing lasts forever though, and like it or not, if you keep sailing west across the Atlantic, you will eventually come to the Caribbean Sea. The decision was no longer when, but where should they make landfall? As Skip looked at his navigation charts, he decided that the best place for them, and right on their course was the small and rarely visited place called Union Island. In fact, it was so rarely visited that when Skip presented the ship documents and their passports, the officials didn't believe their last port of call was Gibraltar 19 days earlier. "You expect us to believe that just the two of you sailed that boat all the way across the Atlantic Ocean and this is your first landfall in 19 days? Ha!" the officials said loudly.

"Well, it's true," Skip said proudly. "And here's our ship's logbook to prove it!" There was no denying the logbook was the absolute official document and with a shrug of both shoulders, the passport agent made that familiar sound of, "Thump, thump, stamp, thump, thump, stamp," as he inked his old-fashioned rubber stamp and imprinted both passports welcoming the boys to Union Island.

The Caribbean Sea was filled with beautiful green islands, friendly people, and plenty of fun-filled days of scuba diving, and beach going. But the boys were on edge; for once again they found themselves being chased by the weather. Hurricane season (the same as cyclones but called hurricanes in this part of the world) was only two months away and that didn't give them much time to cross the entire sea, stop at some of the best dive sites, and still make it to the Panama Canal without encountering one of these enormous storms. After only a week in beautiful green Union Island, the boys set sail and headed west. They stopped at the Dutch Antilles, the Venezuelan island of Margarita, and in spite of hearing that it was pirate territory, went out of their way for fuel and provisions in Colombia.

While in Colombia, they were talking to some other local residents about their journey and quest to find Hina. They explained how they had sailed almost all the way around the world searching for, and trying to catch up to Hina but had never found him. Then they told the story of how they had decided to leave their quest behind and take the advice of the man-eating Dorkus, and wise old Orin, and stop trying to find Skip's brother. They hoped someday they would run into Hina but weren't going to make a life out of the chase. As Skip told the tale, and described Hina and his crescent moon birthmark, he saw the eyes of one of the local fisherman grow big. "Si! Chico Luna!" whispered the fisherman. "Chico Luna was here in Colombia!" The Moon Boy was well known and this fisherman swore he had seen Hina, but said he had got in with some pirates and gone north to Cuba. Skip and Kanek talked about starting their quest again, but decided they were better off without the chase. Although Kanek suspected Skip wasn't really saying how he truly felt, he was happy to live the relaxed life without the danger of trying to find Hina. They agreed it might be in their future, but for now, they were enjoying living a pretty normal life without pursuing Hina.

They successfully made it through the Caribbean without any hurricanes and before they knew it, were dropping their anchor in Colon, the northern end of the Panama Canal. "I always thought that the Panama Canal went from east to west," Kanek said as he was looking at the charts. "But we're actually going to be traveling from north to south, and after two days in the canal, we'll be further south from where we started." The boys pondered the charts and sure enough, Kanek was right.

CHAPTER 21—
OPEN THE GATES!

P reparations to go through the gargantuan Panama Canal were underway. The boys hung car tires wrapped in plastic over the sides to prevent damage in case they bumped into the giant 100-foot tall cement sides of the locks. They padded the solar panels with cushions, removed the dinghy, its motor, and anything else that could be damaged if the boat were to lose control and slam into the walls. The locks are water elevators. The boat enters into the first lock, the gates close, and the lock is flooded with a million gallons of water. As the lock fills, the boat rises to the level of the next lock. As the boat moves into the next lock, its giant gates swing shut, the water floods in and again raises the boat to the next level. That happens three times going up and three times going back down and allows boats to travel through the land portions of Panama that are higher than sea level.

While the boys understood the process, they were not prepared for the reality of it all. The afternoon of their assigned day to enter the canal, Roberto, an official local canal guide came aboard and directed Skip to steer JULIA for the first lock. By the time they entered, it was already dark and the bright artificial lighting cast an eerie glow over the whole scene. There was a huge green neon arrow pointing to the entrance and as Skip steered JULIA into the giant lock, which was easily the size of a football field, they saw there was already a huge container ship in the lock right in front of them. As Roberto said, "Closer, closer, move up closer," Skip and Kanek stared warily at the enormous 3-blade propeller of the ship, not more than 100 feet in front of them. Once they got JULIA tied up in the center of the lock, warning bells rang, the giant steel gates closed behind them with a loud "thud," and the water began to flood the lock. Suddenly it was like JULIA was being torn at from all sides. The lines creaked as they strained at the cleats and Skip fought with the currents that tried to throw their boat against the sharp barnacle covered cement walls. Even with all of Skip's sailing experience, he felt he wasn't in control and sweat dripped off his face in the warm moist tropical air. Kanek was already dripping from working so hard at handling the lines.

The Panama Canal waters tossed their little boat around like a cork in a bathtub!

After a few minutes of turbulence they had been lifted over 50 feet in the water elevator. The chaotic waters calmed down and loud bells rang from all sides as the massive steel gates opened in front of them. At the same time, the propeller on the ship in front began turning slowly at first, then faster and faster, making a new river of current to fight. It went against all of Skip's experience and training to be so close to the ship in front of them, but he had to trust the guide and did as he was told. The men on the top of the locks followed with the lines still attached and helped ease JULIA into the next lock. "Whew, that was fun," Skip joked sarcastically.

"Good, glad you enjoyed it" said Roberto, "because here we go again!" Once more, the gates closed, the lock filled, the waters swirled, the boys struggled to hold their position, and then just as before, the raging waters calmed and they moved to the next lock. They repeated the exhausting process one more time until they had reached the lake level, 85 feet higher than where they had begun. The elevator had done its job. Once they had reached the huge manmade Gatun Lake, the body of water between the up and down locks, Roberto guided them to a peaceful anchorage where they all fell into an exhausted sleep for the night.

"Hurry, we must move quickly," Roberto said as he went around waking the boys. "We have an appointment at the next set of locks and first we must cross the entire 21 mile lake!" As no sails were allowed anywhere on the lake or in the canal, Skip started the engine and they took off at a good clip headed for the three locks which would lower them back to sea level. The bright red sun was already heating up the jungle around them and the animals were coming to life. They heard monkeys screeching, birds squawking, and a deep roar they didn't recognize, but which made them happy they were on a boat and not ashore in the jungle! There must have been a million different shades of green thought Skip as he looked ashore at the incredible variety of plants, shrubs, trees and vines. It was the thickest looking jungle he had ever seen.

They were a few minutes early for their appointed time and so they motored around in circles waiting for the radio call from the controller. Before too long, the call came indicating they should enter the first lock. This time, instead of the lock filling with water though, it drained as if pulling the plug in a bathtub. Aside from a bit of swirling of water, it was nowhere near as difficult as going up had been, and the boys breathed a sigh of relief. Once they were in the third lock, as they were being lowered to sea level, Skip said, "Well Kanek, this is it. In a minute, we'll be back in home waters." Kanek didn't answer. The bells rang and the colossal steel gates swung open. There, in front of them was the Pacific Ocean. It seemed more blue and peaceful than they remembered it. Kanek rubbed his eyes as he looked first at Skip, then at the mighty ocean in front of them.

"You okay? Skip asked. Still Kanek didn't answer.

"Kanek?" Kanek wouldn't look at Skip.

"Kanek!" "Yeah, yeah, what do you want?" Kanek answered with a cracked voice. "Kanek, what's the matter?" He had Skip's attention now.

"It's just, well, now, um, where to from here? Are you sending me back to Tahiti?" Skip always was the the emotional one and it wasn't unusual for him to have tears in his eyes. But this was different seeing Kanek with tears running down his cheeks.

"Well, I don't know Kanek."

"You're the skipper, you're supposed to know everything. How come on this one thing you don't have an answer? Huh? Huh?"

Skip didn't know how to answer so he didn't say anything. He hadn't realized this decision was coming up so fast.

"I know the answer," said Kanek. "You already said it once before so I know what you're going to say. You're going to realize you don't need me because you're not looking for Hina anymore. Hina, Hina, Hina, that's all I've heard about for so long, I'm sick of it. I don't ever want to hear his name again!"

CHAPTER 22— WHICH WAY?

There was something very familiar feeling about the Pacific, as if they were on home-turf. Except of course that it wasn't turf at all, it was water. "Well Kanek, we have a big decision to make. If we continue west, we'll end up back in Tahiti where we met. You'll be back home and can make a life for yourself. If we turn north, we'll end up back in California where I'm from. I should go back to school I guess. Then I can show every one of the bullies that I sailed around the world and they won't bother me anymore. And if I can handle pirates, I know I can handle those bullies. Or we can go east and look for Hina. It's a big decision Kanek, which direction should we go?"

Where to?

"Skip, do you really care about the bullies back home? What are you trying to prove to them? That you're smarter, stronger, tougher than they are? You've proved that to yourself and to me a hundred times over. When are you going to let go and live for you?"

The boys had each matured a lot. They looked at priorities differently than they had before. They had grown by leaps and bounds in their understanding of how to handle tough decisions by putting their priorities in place. What was most important to each of them at this point? Skip had nobody back in California except his nutty aunt Beatrice; not a very tempting option. But he could go back to school and grow up with the rest of the kids his age, and they wouldn't tease him anymore as he now had muscles and wasn't afraid of anything or anybody. Maybe he could even go to a different school and make new friends.

Kanek had grown too and he knew what was important to him— something he hadn't had in a long time—family. Except he had no family to go back to, no place to live, and felt he would be treated as an outsider if he went back to Tahiti because he had been gone so long.

"I don't want to go back to Tahiti," Kanek said. "I just can't go back there, I won't go back there. I've seen too much of the world to go back to living on an island again. Sure, it's beautiful, but it's not as exciting as being out in the bigger world. And Skip, there's no one there for me, they'd put me in a foster home. You're my only family now."

"What did you say?" asked Skip.

"I said you're my family now. You're the closest I'll ever have to a brother Skip."

Trying to understand this, Skip let what Kanek said sink in. "You could come home with me!" Skip exclaimed. "We can both live in California and go to school together. How does that sound?"

"Yeah, I guess that sounds okay," Kanek stammered without much enthusiasm. "It's just that I kind of thought this boat *was* our home."

"It is home. Until we get home, right? I mean, isn't home in California? Okay, it's settled then, we'll turn north for California," Skip said as he gripped the wheel. He looked at Kanek who was staring at him holding his breath waiting for he didn't know what. *"Turn north to go home,"* Skip mumbled to himself, but he didn't turn the wheel. Then suddenly Skip said, "Kanek, take the wheel." Kanek took over the steering while Skip went below. He came up a few minutes later holding a clear bottle with a cork pushed firmly into the top. Inside were a bunch of rolled up papers.

"What's that, Skip?" Kanek's voice was shaking for he just couldn't read his friend's mind this time.

"That is Hina," Skip answered defiantly. "And the Nami Nami maps. I've had it with this mystery person running our lives. I realize now he's just another bully and I don't like bullies. He's been directing my life all the way around the world, and he's preventing me from being who I want to be. You helped me realize this Kanek. Thank you."

"So that's it? Asked Kanek.

"Yep, that's it." And before Kanek could say Nami Nami, Skip heaved the bottle overboard. "Let someone else find it and take on all the troubles the Nami Nami maps cause."

Kanek couldn't believe what he just saw happen, and all he could nervously say was, "What's our new course Skipper?" Skip stared out to sea. He kept gazing for what seemed like the longest time, as if he was in a trance. "Skip?" Kanek questioned? "Skip, are you okay?" He waited and waited until finally Skip turned and faced Kanek. He was smiling as he spoke.

"Kanek, you're right. This IS our home. And I do need you."

Kanek waited breathlessly for the course. And waited…and waited… until finally Skip spoke.

"Turn to course one eight zero," Skip said with the most captain-like voice Kanek had heard yet.

Kanek looked at the compass, started to turn the wheel, but then stopped and said, "But Skipper, that's south, 180 degrees is due south. That wasn't one of our choices and we don't know what's down there at all."

Skip shrugged his shoulders, and looked Kanek in the eye with a smile. "That's right, turn to course 180 degrees Kanek. This search is over. I have already found my brother and I'm looking at him. Let's go find some good things in the world."

You mean it?!" shouted Kanek. "Aye aye Skipper! 180 degrees south. Let's Go!"

"Let's Go!" echoed Skip.

From below, Mango squawked loudly, "Let's Go!, Let's Go! Let's Go!"

The End. For now....

SKIP & KANEK

GLOSSARY

Everything has a specific name on a boat. This prevents confusion and improves communication. It's also a whole new language to learn. For example, if you were to say, "Ease the port jib sheet," your crew would know to "Let out the line on the port side that controls the angle of the jib sail." Take note of the drawing below and you'll easily learn the language of boating. And think of how impressed your friends will be!

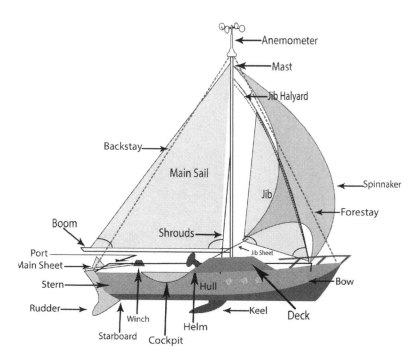

Alternator: Small electrical generator attached to an engine and turned by a rubber belt, which produces electricity. Electricity is necessary to keep the engine running. Cars have them too.

Anemometer: Instrument that measures wind speed by using a wind vane at top of the mast.

Block and tackle: Pulleys and line used to make it easier to lift or pull something. The "purchase power" or added ease of lifting depends on the number of times the line goes back and forth through a series of pulleys.

Bommie: A large coral head, usually big and sharp enough to do serious damage, including putting a hole into a boat.

Boom: Horizontal beam that attaches to the mast and holds the bottom (foot) of the sail in place.

Bow: Front of the boat

Bucked and bobbed, listed, and lurched, broached and yawed: Bounced up and down quickly, then slowly, leaned over, jumped forward, turned sideways to the waves, and pivoted side to side.

Celestial navigation: Finding one's position on earth by measuring the location and angle of the sun and stars relative to your boat at a given time. The instrument used to measure this angle is called a **sextant**.

Chafe gear: Thick leather or canvas that prevent lines from wearing through in one place from continued use.

Cockpit: Area of the boat where one sits to steer, adjust the sails, and relax with lunch.

Deck: Area on which one stands that can be the roof of the cabin. The **mast** is usually attached to the deck as is the rigging.

Face of a wave: Front of a wave that a boat would surf down toward the **trough**.

Forestay: Wire cable connecting the top of the mast to the bow of the boat. This wire cable is critical to holding the mast up. There is also a **backstay** that connects the top of the mast to the stern. **Shrouds** are wire cables that connect the mast to each side of the boat.

Galley: The kitchen on a boat.

Genoa: A large jib.

GPS: Global Positioning System that uses satellites to determine your position anywhere on earth.

Head: The toilet on a boat. Also, the bathroom area is usually called the head.

Helm: Where the steering wheel is located.

Hull: The watertight frame and shell of the boat itself. The actual boat part of the boat. The **cockpit** is in the boat. The mast sticks up from the **Deck** of the boat.

Jib: Sail that is just forward of the mast. Jibs are triangular in shape and come in a variety of sizes to be used in various weather conditions. A storm jib is a very small version for heavy weather.

Jibe: Significantly change direction of the boat while sailing downwind. All sails must be changed to the other side of the boat in order to keep them filled with wind.

Keel: Heavy low part of the boat that sticks down into the water. Keeps the boat upright and prevents it from slipping sideways.

Knot: Nautical measure of speed. A knot is 1.15 miles per hour, or about 15% faster. This applies to the boat's speed and wind speed. Of course, a knot is also what one ties in a line or rope to attach it to another line or just about anything.

Line: See rope and line

Locks: A small section of a canal or other waterway in which the water level can be changed by filling or draining it, to raise and lower boats passing through the canal. Like a water elevator.

Main sheet: The line which controls the angle of the **Mainsail**.

Mainsail: The main sail, which is attached to the mast and boom.

Main Salon: Largest living room type area on a boat. Often used for dining and is usually located in the center area below decks.

Mayday: The highest level of distress signal used by boats and aircraft. It indicates there is an immediate threat to life and is always repeated three times so there is no misunderstanding. Also, the first day of the month of May, which is a holiday in many countries.

Nautical mile: Nautical measure of distance. A nautical mile is 1.15 miles or about 15% further than a standard mile. It's based on knots.

Pod of dolphins: Same as a school of dolphins. A bunch of them.

Port: The left side of a boat when you're facing forward toward the bow. Port has 4 letters and ends in "T," just like Left.

Reef sails: Reducing the size of a sail such as the mainsail or jib, by tucking away, or rolling up a portion of the sail. When the wind comes up strong, sails can be reefed instead of being replaced with a smaller sail, making the boat more manageable in storms.

Rigging: **Standing rigging** is the cables, wires, shackles, and other attachments that keep the mast in place. **Running Rigging** is the lines, pulleys, poles, and gear that control the sails.

Roger: Acknowledgement that you heard and understood what someone said—usually on a radio call, but also can be face to face.

Rope and Line: Any rope becomes a line when it's on a boat. Each line then has a specific name. A **sheet** is a line that controls the angle of a sail, such as the **main sheet** that controls the **mainsail**. A **halyard** is a line that hauls a sail up or down. One might say, "Take up the main halyard," which means to haul up the mainsail. Also, a line can be said such as, "Your hair looks nice today."

Sarcophagus: Burial box for ancient Egyptians. Usually made from stone or marble and decorated with elaborate carvings telling the story of who was buried there.

Sextant: Hand held instrument that measures the angle of the sun and stars above the horizon. By comparing their position to the books which show the stars' positions at certain times of day, one is able to determine your position on the ocean while at sea.

Spinnaker: Large balloon shaped sail that is set out in front of the boat. They are often in bright colors and are very large. While they add speed and stability, these sails require lots of attention.

Squall: Micro-storms found in tropical warm waters in which strong winds of approximately 40-50 knots are common accompanied by heavy rain. Some hit with complete surprise.

Starboard: The right side of a boat when you're facing forward toward the bow.

Stern: Back of the boat

Storm Jib: See Jib

Tack: Significantly change direction of the boat while sailing upwind. All sails must be changed to the other side of the boat in order to keep them filled with wind. Also used to pin something to a bulletin board.

Tether: Strong line with steel clips on both ends. One clip on the person, the other on the boat to prevent falling overboard. Adjustable from short (3 feet) to long (6 feet).

Trough: The low part between ocean swells.

Tuk-tuk: Three-wheel motorized taxis used in Thailand and other Southeast Asian countries.

Toss Your Cookies: To vomit with great explosive power.

VHF Radio: Most commonly used type of radio on boats, which operates by line of sight. Therefore its range is limited to about 20 miles due to the curvature of the earth. For much further distances, a **single side band** radio is used, which bounces signals off of the earth's atmosphere.

Weigh Anchor: To raise the anchor in order to get the boat underway.

Whitecaps: Waves on top of swells that turn white with foam as they build to a peak and then break.

Windlass: Large winch on the bow of the boat used to haul up, and let out the anchor chain. Can be manual or electric.

Winch: A rotating steel drum used to mechanically wind up or let out lines. There are usually multiple winches on a boat, each having a specific use. Winches are used to haul up halyards, anchor chain, to control sheets, or just about any other line that needs the mechanical advantage added by the use of a winch.

Made in the USA
San Bernardino, CA
19 December 2019